the destiny of linus hoppe

the destiny of linus hoppe

le destin de linus hoppe

translated from the french by
catherine temerson

DELACORTE PRESS

Published by
Delacorte Press
an imprint of
Random House Children's Books
a division of Random House, Inc.
New York

Originally published in France in 2001 by Bayard Editions Jeunesse

Library of Congress Cataloging-in-Publication Data
Bondoux, Anne-Laure.
[Destin de Linus Hoppe. English]
The destiny of Linus Hoppe / Anne-Laure Bondoux ;
translated from the French by Catherine Temerson.
p. cm.
Originally published in France in 2001 by Bayard Editions Jeunesse
under title: Le destin de Linus Hoppe.
Summary: In a utopian world, fourteen-year-old Linus, who is approaching the test that will determine which Realm he will live in, rejects the accepted way of life and ventures to change his destiny.
ISBN 0-385-73229-5 (trade) — ISBN 0-385-90255-7 (glb)
[1. Interpersonal relations—Fiction. 2. Science fiction.]
I. Temerson, Catherine. II. Title.
PZ7.B63696De 2005
[Fic]—dc22
2004014456

The text of this book is set in 12.5-point Apollo MT.

Book design by Angela Carlino

Printed in the United States of America

May 2005

10 9 8 7 6 5 4 3 2 1

the destiny of linus hoppe

chapter 1

Linus Hoppe sat on the third level of the Zip, pinching his nose. The other passengers seemed oblivious to the vanilla fragrance that permeated the train car, but Linus couldn't get used to it. The sickly-sweet odor clung to his clothes and, worse, made him feel ill. He knew that something had to be done to cover up the foul-smelling vapors emanating from the subterranean Industrial Zone, but why had vanilla been chosen? Linus couldn't help wondering if the senior managers of the Trans-Urban Company had ever ventured into the transportation system since they'd decided to install the air fresheners.

The train glided noiselessly through the tunnels. Beyond the windows, there was nothing to see for miles, just darkness dotted at regular intervals by the glow of the small light fixtures on the tunnel walls. Back in the early 2000s, the train used to emerge into the open air right after leaving Paris. But today the regulations were much stricter, and any potential blight on the landscape was buried deep underground. The old railroad tracks had become places where people went for leisurely strolls.

Linus flipped open his pocket computer. The trip to

his suburban station lasted twenty minutes, giving him ample time to go over the day's courses.

"Hello, Linus, my little cookie!" the computer blared unexpectedly.

Linus quickly lowered the volume as several people turned to look at him. He smiled at them, slightly embarrassed. Once again Chem had played one of his practical jokes. Not a day went by without Linus's hacker friend tampering with his programs. This time the joke was harmless, but the other day Chem had nearly wrecked Linus's touch-sensitive screen.

"Honestly, Chem," Linus had said to him, "why don't you target someone else?"

Chem had laughed into his scarf. "Anyone else would beat me up!" he'd said. "You're the only one at school who still has a sense of humor!"

Linus sighed. Chem was right: ever since the beginning of the year, the mood in school had deteriorated daily. Students glanced at one another suspiciously, they worked furtively in their own little corners, and classrooms were like battlefields. Not that there was any physical violence; after all, no one wanted to get expelled from the system. Instead the attacks were underhanded, with countless wounds to self-esteem, strings of petty intrigues, psychological bruises, and mental aggressions. In this arena, humor was definitely out of place.

"They're scared stiff," Chem kept grumbling to Linus. "The end-of-year exam is driving them all crazy."

Linus could relate. The end-of-year exam was all he

could think about too. In three months, he was going to be tested by the Great Processor. The outcome would determine his future. A score of 150 or higher guaranteed he would remain in Realm One—where his life would barely change. He'd continue living at home, with his parents and his sister, Mieg, who had scored 185 two years before, and he would pursue his studies in the city. Later on, he'd receive fantastic bank loans to buy a house in the Protected Zone, and he'd be promoted to a position of responsibility, as his parents had. A score of less than 150, on the other hand, would have consequences he couldn't begin to imagine. One thing was certain: he would have to leave his home in the Protected Zone.

But Linus knew he had nothing to fear. With minimal effort, he was always among the top students. He had never had any problems with his teachers, had never been reprimanded, and had hardly ever been absent. According to his parents, the exam was a mere formality.

Still, Linus thought, *accidents happen.*

For several months, the word *accident* had been popping up in his thoughts regularly. The word didn't refer to a concrete reality; it simply sprang to mind unexpectedly, simultaneously frightening and tempting, much like a plane ticket to an exotic destination.

Having been completely absorbed in his thoughts, Linus realized he no longer had time to go over his courses. The train would be stopping in five minutes. He shut down his computer.

"See you soon, Cookie!" mumbled the synthetic voice.

Linus couldn't help smiling. Chem was an unbelievable prankster, but in spite of his jokes, he was also the best friend Linus had at school. The trouble was that by overplaying the rebel, Chem risked not being admitted into the best realm. Everyone knew that insubordinates were sent to Realm Three, where they endured a special treatment—one that involved a mixture of iron discipline and bullying. The ones who knuckled under were reevaluated, with the luckier ones reinstated in Realm One. As for the others, no one knew what became of them. But the teachers' threats had no effect on Chem's attitude. He persisted in folding his arms and smiling arrogantly. When Linus expressed worry, Chem boasted, "I can do whatever I want with the Great Processor. Don't forget, Cookie, I'm a computer genius! If I choose to, I can bust its circuits!"

Looking out the window, Linus caught sight of the halo of light from the approaching station. He shook his head. Of course, Chem was bragging. No one had ever succeeded in outwitting the Great Processor.

Linus buttoned up his jacket, put his computer away in his backpack, and headed to the first level of the train. The doors swished open and Linus stepped out onto the platform. No more vanilla scent here. He could breathe through his nose again. Relieved, he swiped his ID card through the slot at the gate.

"ID: Linus Hoppe. Authorized access into the Protected Zone. Good evening," said the electronic voice at the gate. Making his way through the crowd, Linus headed toward the elevators.

"Hey, Linus!" a familiar voice called to him from behind.

It was Mieg, his big sister, coming home from school too. She caught up with him, smiling and happy as usual. Over her long curly black hair, she wore a red hat with the insignia of the HIA, the Higher Institute of Architecture.

"Did you have a good day?" she asked, kissing Linus on the cheek.

"Not particularly good or bad. There were no fries at the cafeteria, poor Iona got another lousy grade in biotech, that moron Rodrigo made Marny cry, and Chem fiddled with my programs again. Routine, as you can see."

Mieg frowned. "You're very blasé for a fourteen-year-old!"

Linus shrugged. The elevator had arrived. They were pushed along by the crowd cramming into it.

"Unlike you," Mieg said, "I was very excited the year of my exam. I worked hard, but it was fascinating. You don't seem to realize how much it's worth the effort."

Linus looked down at his feet and all the feet around his. From the shoes alone, he could tell that the people surrounding him lived in the Protected Zone. Theirs was the simple, clean, and comfortable footwear of the elite.

"Are you listening to me?" Mieg asked, slightly annoyed.

"Sorry, I'm tired."

The elevator doors opened. Again, Linus let himself be carried by the flow of humanity, happy to breathe the cold, dry air outside.

"You'll take a restorative bath when we get home," Mieg said, adjusting her hat. "Then I'll make you one of my tasty vitamin-enriched shakes. Okay?"

Linus nodded. He started walking along the edge of the sidewalk, his nose in the air. Between the bare branches of the trees, he saw that the winter moon was rising. Everything was quiet. The only sounds were the clicks of window shutters being rolled down, the mewing of a cat, laughter, and the notes of a piano coming from an artist's residence.

"There's no better place on earth. Don't you agree?" Mieg murmured as she noticed that Linus's mind was elsewhere.

They walked the rest of the way in silence, each appreciating the artificial serenity of the Protected Zone.

Immersed up to his neck in the warm bath, his eyes half shut, Linus surrendered to the feeling of well-being. His parents hadn't come home yet, but the delicious smell of roast chicken wafted up from the kitchen and seeped under the door. The oven, which switched itself on automatically, had been carefully programmed so that the Hoppe family could sit down to dinner at 8:30 p.m.

Mieg had put on some music, and the soothing sounds of the sitar added to the relaxed atmosphere in the house.

In the bathroom, the leaves of the green plants were now covered with tiny drops of humidity. Only the twitter of birds was missing or Linus would have been convinced he was somewhere deep in the equatorial jungle. *How is it possible to feel unhappy in this setting?* he wondered. He wanted to reply that it was impossible, but he hesitated. Mieg had made her choice long ago. She would go far; that was what her teachers predicted. They already felt certain she would be admitted into the Order of Great Builders, the world-renowned brotherhood of architects.

"What about me?" Linus asked himself. "What great things do I feel like accomplishing? And who said I had to accomplish great things at all?"

"Knock, knock!" Mieg said suddenly, behind the door. "I'm bringing you your vitamin-enriched shake."

Linus gathered foam over his body. "Come in," he said.

Mieg entered the bathroom, wheeling a serving cart that bore a glass filled with an apple green liquid.

"Taste this! I've improved it again!" she said, proudly.

Linus remained motionless in the water, as though trapped in a coffin of foam.

"Thanks," he said. "I'll drink it. Now would you mind leaving?"

"Oh, excuse me." Mieg chuckled. "I forgot that Mr. Linus doesn't like to be seen naked anymore."

Linus scowled. "So? That's my privilege, isn't it?"

"It certainly is," Mieg replied, though that didn't prevent her from sitting on the edge of the bathtub. "You've become so prudish recently. You don't even tell me about your crushes anymore. I guess I'm no longer your confidante?"

"There's nothing to tell you about."

"You're not in love?"

"No, I'm not! Please leave!"

"Too bad. I thought that might explain your mood swings." Mieg gathered some foam in one hand and threw it at her brother's face. Then she left, laughing.

Linus wiped his forehead and sat up. Mieg had always interfered in things that were none of her business. It was true that Linus used to tell her everything. But now, he managed just fine on his own. How could Mieg even think he was in love? Him? Not a chance! The girls in his class were either unpleasant, stupid, or too pretty to be interested in him. No use getting carried away.

Linus swallowed the contents of the glass. The shake tasted slightly bitter, but was very refreshing. In addition to all her intellectual qualities, Mieg had always shown an undeniable talent for innovative recipes. "There's no doubt about it; she's perfect!" Linus said. "She truly belongs in Realm One."

When he left the bathroom ten minutes later, Linus heard his father's voice below in the living room. He quickly got dressed and headed down to join him. Mr. Hoppe was having a conversation with Linus's grandmother, whose round, suntanned face was displayed on the family computer's giant screen.

"Hi, Dad!" Linus called out. Then, waving at the screen, he added, "Hi, Grandma!"

"Hello, darling!" Grandma said, smiling. "How are you?"

"I'm okay."

"Your classes?"

"Okay."

"You could be a bit more talkative," his father broke in, looking askance at him. "Did you have a bad day?"

Linus sighed. "I'm just tired."

"You should come out here to see me," Grandma said as she shifted on the screen. "The Florida sunshine and fresh air would do you good."

"Come on, Mom!" Mr. Hoppe interrupted her. "You

know full well Linus can't go away. His exam is in three months! Afterward, we'll see."

Grandma looked exasperated. "If it were up to me," she said, "I would abolish the whole thing, and no one would ever ruin their health taking the exam!"

"Maybe so," Linus's father snapped back, "but then you'd have to reform all of society, and you're the one whose health would suffer. Anyhow, Linus will do well. That's not a problem. He'll go spend his vacation with you if you want."

"All the same," Grandma said, "in my day, no one was ranked by the Great Processor and—"

"And life was certainly no better!"

Linus left the room, tired of hearing the same old conversation between his father and grandmother. Yes, he'd probably spend his vacation in Florida, and the air would be good for him. Unless, of course, an "accident" happened first.

With a mocking smile, Linus entered the kitchen just as the oven bell went off, signaling the end of the cooking time. The chicken was roasted; his father shut down the computer; his mother's keys jingled in the foyer; it was time to sit down for dinner.

chapter 3

"Maybe it was my shake!" Mieg said as she hovered over Linus, who was doubled up in pain in bed. "He was so worn out last night. I mixed together a lot of things."

"Linus," Mrs. Hoppe said, "where does it hurt? Is it your stomach?"

Linus groaned. As his mother stroked his forehead and straightened his pillow, he clenched his teeth and grimaced.

"I'm so sorry, little brother," Mieg said. "So sorry."

Linus's father, still in pajamas in spite of the late hour, came into the room, a sheet of paper in his hand.

"I consulted the poison control center Web site," he said. "If this is Mieg's complete list of ingredients, Linus couldn't have been poisoned."

"Phew!" Mieg sighed.

"But I don't feel well!" Linus complained.

"Well, you'll just stay here this morning, where it's nice and warm," Mr. Hoppe instructed. "As for me, I'd better get going."

"Me too," Mrs. Hoppe said. "I have an important meeting, but I'll be back at noon. In the meantime, if you don't mind, dear, I'll give you an analgesic. I'll call the school and explain. After all, it's the first time this year you've missed a day. They won't make a fuss. And besides, it's Friday."

Mieg, already muffled up in her coat, kissed Linus on the forehead. "You were probably already coming down with something yesterday. That's why you weren't yourself."

Linus didn't answer. He closed his eyes. In a moment, he would be alone, in peace and quiet. With everyone gone, he'd have the whole morning to think things over . . . and to decide on a course of action.

His mother came in, an aspirin patch in one hand and her leather attaché case in the other. Linus stuck the patch on his arm.

"Will you be all right?" his mother asked as she slipped on her shoes.

"Uh-huh."

"Are you sure?"

"I'm sure. I'm just going to sleep."

Mrs. Hoppe glanced at her wristwatch, kissed her son, then disappeared. Linus heard her close the front door and lock up. The light of the security system in the hallway turned green. Linus got up. He put on a sweater and a pair of socks, took off the patch, and went down to the kitchen for something to eat. He felt fine. It was the first time he'd faked being sick. The idea had come to him when his alarm clock had gone off. For some reason, he'd suddenly felt the need to escape from the daily grind—train, school, teachers, classmates, crowds—the whole destructive whirlwind that prevented a person from thinking. A new word loomed before him, like a wall at the back of a dead-end street: *destiny*. And it seemed to him the word deserved a morning's consideration.

Linus went into the living room. Like all self-respecting Realm One citizens, his parents owned a size-able library. The books, neatly lined up, were chosen for the harmonious colors of their spines rather than their content. These days there were just so many other ways of obtaining information. Linus was the only one in the family who ever upset the calculated layout of the books by dipping into one of them at random. But today there was nothing random about his choice: the first volume of the encyclopedic dictionary. He put it on the table and looked up the definition of his word.

> **DESTINY** (n.)—**1.** According to certain beliefs, the power thought to predetermine the course of events irrevocably. **2.** The set of events that make up the life of a human being, viewed as resulting from causes independent of that person's will. **3.** The course of existence, viewed as capable of being changed by the person living it.

Linus looked out the window. The street was de-serted, clean, as orderly as the room of a model child. If the wind hadn't been stirring the branches of the trees and blowing around the last dead leaves, he could have sworn he was looking at a photo. "That's strange," Linus said. "The definitions are contradictory. First it says you can't have any effect on your destiny, then it says you can change its 'course.'" He went back to the dictionary and looked up *accident*.

> **ACCIDENT** (n.)—**1.** An unexpected, fortuitous, unpredictable event. **2.** An unexpected, sudden event that involves damage and danger.

Damage and danger. Linus suddenly realized he'd never experienced an accident. For as far back as he could remember, he'd never been in an unexpected situation. How was that possible? Chem had known difficult times; he'd suffered. Maybe that was why he appeared so detached from everything. But as far as Linus was concerned, nothing. His life had unfolded in a linear fashion, faultlessly, along the dotted lines.

Deeply puzzled, Linus put the dictionary back on the shelf and went up to his room. He switched on his computer and logged on to the WEF, the Worldwide Exchange Forum. He typed in the subject he wanted to talk about—*Accident*—and his message:

Seeking correspondent (preferably around fourteen years old, living in France) who has had one or more accidents, and who can tell me how this has affected their life.

Linus added his e-mail address and sent his message. Now he simply had to wait for responses.

chapter 4

At eleven-thirty in the morning, Linus received several messages in answer to his request. They came from as far away as Istanbul, Madrid, and Warsaw. An Italian told him about how he'd been hit by a car back in the days when those vehicles used to speed through the cities; a Polish woman described her skiing accident in detail. Disappointed, Linus decided to reformulate his request when another correspondent logged on.

Hello evry one! I liv in a suburbin zone. I'm forteen, My name is Yosh, My axident hapened when I was 2. My mother told me somthing brok inside my head. A vain, I dont know exactly. My mother sez thats what made me stupid. Since then I hav trouble in scool. It's becoz of my axident.

Linus had to control himself to keep from laughing at the number of spelling mistakes. It was unbelievable. He'd never read anything like it. Yosh had to be the laughingstock in his school.

"Here's someone who's going to get flunked by the Great Processor!" he said.

However, his curiosity was aroused. He reread the message more carefully. Yosh might not be as stupid as

Linus thought. He was the only one who'd really answered the question. Linus was about to ask him for more information when the light of the security system in the hallway turned red. He heard his mother entering the house. Quickly he typed, *Hello, Yosh! I'd like to stay in touch, but I can't write more just now. Talk to you tonight!*

He shut down his computer and dove into bed, where he buried his head under the quilt and pretended to be asleep. A few seconds later, his mother very quietly opened the door to his room.

"Are you sleeping, Linus?" she whispered.

Since he didn't answer, Mrs. Hoppe shut the door and tiptoed away. Knowing her, Linus figured she had brought work home, and he was sure she wouldn't come up to check on him for another few hours. So he threw off his quilt and folded his arms behind his neck.

"What is my destiny?" he wondered aloud. "Can I still change things? What about Chem? And Yosh?" Everything seemed to happen as though history had already been written. He saw this clearly for the first time. But more important, for the first time, he saw his future staring him straight in the face, prefabricated, spoon-fed, as insipid as soy steak.

Linus started laughing. Several scenarios flashed before his eyes:

Scenario 1: Linus at twenty. He'd grown and was now taller than his father. He'd also just graduated from law school with honors. Thanks to a bank loan, he was buying office space and opening a law firm. By asking for a legal dispensation, he was able to continue living with his parents until he earned a high enough income to live on his own.

Scenario 2: Linus at thirty. As a famous attorney, he earned a great deal of money, spent his vacation in Mexico, and planned on getting married. His future wife looked like a younger version of his mother, and she too was brilliant and practiced yoga.

Scenario 3: Linus at forty. His law firm was so prosperous, he no longer needed to go to the office. A young staff did the work for him. His two children (one boy and one girl, the ideal number) got the highest grades in school. They would eventually appear before the Great Processor and start the cycle all over again.

"Stop!" Linus shouted.

Though he was lying in bed, Linus had the unpleasant feeling of being on a never-ending merry-go-round ride. Of being screwed down on the merry-go-round like a wooden horse. Each time it went around, he thought the scenery had changed, and hoped to get off, but that never happened. Nothing changed. It was impossible to get off, and the heady music of the merry-go-round ended up making the horse dizzy. He kept going round and round, heading strictly nowhere.

"Unless an 'axident' occurs," Linus said, thinking of Yosh's spelling of the word.

According to the dictionary, accidents were chance occurrences. Did that mean a premeditated event couldn't be called an accident?

"I'm going to change the course of my destiny," Linus declared. "And I've got three months to arrange it."

chapter 5

"You're nuts" was all Chem said to Linus the following Monday.

They were outside, sitting on a frost-covered bench in the school courtyard. The other students had opted to spend their recreation period inside, in the weight room, or in front of screens in the multimedia library.

"I thought you'd understand," Linus said, lowering his head. "You're always saying you reject the system."

"I reject it for myself!" Chem said. "But for you, it would be really stupid."

"Why?"

"Because, Cookie . . . it just would be. If I were you, I'd stop thinking about this crap."

"Crap? I'm disappointed in you, Chem. I thought you were real. You're nothing but a big talker."

Linus got up, turned his back on Chem, and headed toward the cafeteria.

"Wait!" Chem called to him. "I'm coming to eat with you."

"No way. We're through talking."

Chem caught up with Linus and grabbed him by the arm. "Let's say it isn't crap. Let's say I understand you and I'm willing to help. So let's eat together, Linus, and you'll tell me what's been going on inside your head since last week, okay?"

Linus stared at his friend with mistrust. Chem was four inches taller than Linus, and with his extra-large jacket and two scarves wound around his neck, Chem looked like an old-time lumberjack. In comparison, Linus appeared as frail as a miniature fir tree.

Linus gave in. "Okay. But promise to listen without interrupting."

"I swear!" Chem said, his hand on his heart.

It was warm in the cafeteria. Chem unwound one of his scarves, leaving the other on, as he always did. People who knew him were used to this. But Linus still remembered the day he'd kidded Chem and asked him why he never took off his second scarf. It had been the middle of June, not exactly cold-catching weather. "Do you really want to see what's underneath?" Chem had said, curtly.

Before Linus had had time to answer, Chem had raised the edge of his scarf. Linus had felt himself turning pale. Chem's neck was one enormous puffy white scar.

Months later Chem told him the story behind it. One night, when Chem was five, a fire broke out at his house. He almost escaped uninjured, except that as he ran for safety, he got entangled in a burning curtain. After months in the hospital, and two operations, he went back to a normal life. However, nothing was as it had been before.

The fire destroyed Chem's house, and his family had to

start again from scratch. To make matters worse, Chem's parents were held responsible for the accident and prohibited by the Higher Court from having another child. For Chem, who'd dreamed of having a little sister, this ruling had been like an open wound and remained so.

Sitting opposite Chem, Linus ate in silence.

"So?" Chem asked.

"I'm thinking about your accident."

"Nice of you to think about it. I'm doing everything I can to forget it."

"I met a guy on the WEF. His name is Yosh. He said he had an accident when he was little. I spent the weekend talking about it with him."

"Well, now I understand what made you depressed, my poor Linus!"

"You promised not to interrupt."

"Sorry."

"Will you let me have my say?"

"I will. You're not eating your cheese?"

"Chem! Take the cheese and be quiet."

"Thanks. And, by the way, enjoy your meal!"

"From what he said, Yosh had a brain lesion when he was two years old. He has no idea how it happened; the only thing he knows is he almost died. He survived, but the physicians told his parents he'd be mentally retarded."

"Real cheery!" Chem blurted out.

Linus glared at him. "Yosh's parents took care of him but always treated him like an infant. In fact, the aftereffects of the lesion weren't all that bad. He was able to walk again, recovered his speech, and was even admitted to school. But I don't think his parents are very smart; they keep treating him like a retard. Of course, Yosh does have language problems—though I've only seen his e-mail. It's loaded with mistakes—you can't even imagine. Still, Yosh isn't stupid. He spends his time online, on the WEF, networking with people from all over the world. He knows a lot of stuff. At school he's often behind because he's slow. We spoke about the exam. He says if he can get into Realm Two, he'll be really pleased."

"Good. So?" Chem asked, taking a sip of water.

"So, I'd like to be in his shoes."

Chem choked. "In the shoes of a retard?"

"But I'm telling you, he isn't a retard! I'm sure if he had parents like mine, a house like mine, and lived like me, he'd do as well as me!"

"Keep dreaming," Chem said, wiping up water from the table.

"In any case, that's not the point. I'd just like to change the course of my destiny."

Chem whistled through his teeth. "Is that all, Cookie?"

"Look, you told me you could bust the Great Processor's circuits. I'm not asking you to go that far. I'd just like you to change my score on the day of the exam. I don't want to stay in Realm One."

"Is that all?"

"Well . . . yes. That's all."

Chem leaned way back and started laughing. His cheeks got red. The students at the other tables started looking at him disapprovingly.

"You've really taken me for a ride, Linus," Chem said, shaking his head. "This is the best joke I've heard in years."

"But I'm dead serious!" Linus said, annoyed. He leaned forward and stared Chem straight in the eye. "So, Mr. Hotshot, can you help or not?"

Chem's face clouded over. "You're nuts," he mumbled. "Really nuts." Then he sighed. "It's crazy, but I'll think about it. And you'd better think about it too. The rest of your life depends on it, Cookie."

That night, before dinner, Linus went back online with Yosh. Millions of questions about Realm Two crowded his mind. But cautiously, he typed only, *Hi, Yosh, what's new with you?*

Twenty seconds later an answer flashed onscreen.

Today I saw my psicologist. She gets on my nerves. She mayks me play childrin's games. I told her ages ago it bors me! What about you, do you have a psicologist too?

No, Linus replied. *Apparently I don't need one. Though these days . . . Fortunately, I have my friend Chem. He's stubborn as a mule, but he still listens to me. Why don't you just tell the psychologist to go jump in the lake?*

I'm oblyged to see her, Yosh replied. *She seyz if I dont, I'll be sent to liv in the madhouse. Its becoze of my temper tantrums. I have dredful temper tantrums. For example, I thro my things out the windo. When they fall from the sixth floor, the naybors are anoyed!*

Linus swallowed. It occurred to him that Yosh might be loony.

What triggers your temper tantrums? he asked.

Lots of things! Yosh wrote back. *Speshially when I see my parents. Their unhapy and alwais tired from their work.*

I think its crumy to work in the industrial zone, but they hav no choice. Its like me and the psicologist.

"Who are you online with?" Mieg asked, coming into Linus's room.

Linus gave a start and turned around, furious. "You could knock on the door before entering, you know!"

"I just came to tell you dinner is ready," Mieg said, craning her neck to see her brother's computer screen. "Another one of your little secrets? Really, Linus, you sure have changed."

"Must be my age," Linus replied, ironically. "Please get out of my room. I'll be right down."

Mieg left, looking hurt. Linus instantly felt guilty, but Mieg was the last person he wanted to divulge his plans to. He sent Yosh a final message of encouragement, wished him good night, and made a WEF appointment for the next day. Then he went down to dinner, trying to look like his usual dynamic, self-confident, and well-adjusted self. A teenager with excellent prospects.

During the meal, the conversation turned to a party the Higher Institute of Architecture students were throwing in a month and a half. Mieg, whose class was in charge of decorating the reception room, was enthusiastically describing the colors of the fresco she had painted on one of the walls for the occasion.

"We can't wait to see it," their mother said.

"I'll bring a camera," their father added. "Then we can post the photo on the Internet. Your work may get noticed by a professional. Wouldn't that be nice?"

Linus looked at his parents and sister with curiosity. They seemed so happy and so confident. Suddenly he asked, "Why is everything so easy for us?"

His question was met with silence.

"What do you mean?" Mrs. Hoppe finally asked him.

Linus put his napkin down on the table and started folding it as he spoke. "What I mean is, things don't always turn out well for everyone. Some hardworking people have problems with their neighbors or have children who don't do well in school."

Mr. Hoppe frowned. "Are you trying to tell us you got a bad grade, Linus?"

"No, that's not the point! I'd just like to understand why everyone doesn't have the same life as us. Mom and you both like your work, you earn a lot of money, you live in a safe neighborhood, you—"

"You sound as if you're blaming us," his mother said, indignantly.

"Let Linus speak!" Mieg broke in. "You keep interrupting him!"

The dish of vegetables in the middle of the table was getting cold. Linus stared blankly at the slices of squash. He was thinking about Yosh, wondering how dinnertime was at his house. After another long silence, Linus mumbled, "I could also throw a temper tantrum. A 'dredful' one."

He could feel Mieg's and his parents' eyes on him. They obviously didn't comprehend what was going on. He asked, "Why don't people in Realm One ever mix with people from Realm Two?"

His father cleared his throat and wiped the corners of his mouth. "That's the way society is structured, Linus. Some people are capable of running things, making important decisions, coming up with new ideas, or . . . painting frescoes. Others don't have these abilities. They may be good at more physical, manual tasks. It's a fair exchange and an equitable division of labor. Ranking people for the different realms makes things easier. It saves time for everyone concerned."

Mrs. Hoppe sighed. "Personally, I think you're worried about being tested by the Great Processor. That's normal; it's a decisive event. We've all been through it."

Linus stared at her. He knew he had no right to question his mother about the exam. It was an unspoken fact that everyone learned at a young age: no one ever discussed the exam in detail. Adults almost seemed to have forgotten the whole experience, as though the exam itself wasn't all that important. Nonetheless Linus asked, "When you were my age, were you afraid of being admitted into Realm Two?"

"Of course! I was worried sick!" his mother said.

"Why?"

"Because I'd have found it unbearable to be . . . somewhere else, in an unknown place, with people who were too different from me. As soon as the realms were created, my parents were given the right to live in the Protected Zone. This is where I grew up—like you, like Mieg. I knew I belonged in Realm One, and I did everything to remain in it."

Linus rested his chin in his hands. He wanted to end the conversation. His head was swirling with too many contradictory thoughts. Still, he forced himself to smile. "The vegetables are getting cold," he said. "Let's finish eating!"

chapter 7

As the weeks went by, the winter weather turned milder. Linus continued corresponding with Yosh on the WEF. They exchanged favorite music and sent each other digital photographs of their rooms and families. Yosh mentioned his temper tantrums several times, explaining that they occurred when he felt frustrated.

Its like a wild beest wants to attak me. My psicologist sez I must not do it. I must calm down. I'd like to, but some times it isnt possibl. I think I'm a lion taymer and I can keep the beest away with my wip.

Linus printed out each e-mail and filed the photos away in an album he carried around with him. At school, he took advantage of a moment when he and Chem were alone in a corner of the multimedia library, far from the other students, to show Chem the album.

"This guy looks weird," Chem said, examining a photo of Yosh.

"Not so weird," Linus replied. "Maybe it's his hairstyle. His mother cuts his hair. They can't afford to go to a barber."

Chem leafed through the album, then looked at Linus

with concern. "Are you sure you want to lead his kind of life?" he asked.

Linus took the album back and put it away in his backpack. He sighed. "No, I'm not sure."

"Then maybe we should rethink your plan?"

Linus shook his head slowly. "No, let's move forward. How are you doing with the software?"

"It's progressing," Chem said. "I got into the database and scrambled things to cover my tracks. It was difficult, but . . ."

"But what?"

"But totally awesome!" Chem was beaming.

Linus gazed around at the desks in the multimedia library. His classmates were working in front of computer terminals, taking notes on their electronic notepads. They had tense, pale faces, nervous tics, and bitten-down fingernails.

For the past several weeks, Linus had stopped studying for his courses. His grades had been slipping, but not dramatically so. He didn't want to attract attention, only to make it look as though this bad patch were due to fatigue.

"I'm going to suggest we meet," Linus said. "I want to see Yosh in the flesh. That's when I'll decide."

Chem nodded. "Since I'm involved in this project, I'd like to meet him too."

"Great." Linus was pleased. "You know, Yosh already knows about you. I sent him the photo we took at your house. Remember? The day we dressed up in your father's old clothes?"

"You sent that picture?" Chem cried out. "You stink! He's going to think I'm the biggest cornball on earth!"

Linus stifled a laugh. "That makes up for all the times you tampered with my computer. Guess it's easy to dish out jokes and hard to have them played on you!"

chapter 8

Two weeks later, Linus and Chem stepped onto a Zip train bound for the southern suburbs.

"What's wrong with you?" Chem asked Linus. "You look like you're having a heart attack. Your face is beet red."

"It's the vanilla scent," Linus said, grimacing. "I can't stand it, so I breathe through my mouth."

Chem shook his head. "I forgot about your delicate constitution, Cookie. Once I took the train when the air fresheners were on the blink, and all I can say is, hurrah for vanilla!"

Since they couldn't find seats, Linus and Chem stood by the doors. It was Saturday afternoon and the train was crowded. Even though the big stores encouraged shoppers to buy online, people still preferred making the rounds of the supermarkets on weekends.

"Do you think people who work in the subterranean Industrial Zone are entitled to air fresheners too?" Linus asked.

"I hope so!"

"Yosh's parents are employed down there," Linus explained. "For all we know, they spend their days in the stench."

"We're going to get there early," Chem noted.

"All the better. That'll give us time to look around. I've never set foot in the Open Zone."

"I have," Chem said. "I have an aunt who lives there. It's more or less like the Protected Zone, except there are more buildings, more concrete, and more noise. And more dogs."

"Yosh mentioned the dogs. His neighbors all have dogs, but his parents don't want any. They say they have their share of problems with a child like Yosh."

The Zip stopped at the central station and loads of people got off. Some jump seats freed up, so Chem and Linus sat down. They fell silent for a while, each absorbed in his own thoughts. Linus was nervous about meeting Yosh. He felt he knew him well from their communications over the World Exchange Forum, but a face-to-face meeting was totally different.

"The other night I found some stuff on the database," Chem said in a low voice. "By matching up the scores and admissions of the last few years, I discovered inconsistencies."

Linus looked at Chem attentively. "You mean the system has flaws?"

Chem nodded. "Like all systems," he whispered. "But what I mean is, we may not be the first people intent on tampering with the exam results. Others before you have already gotten themselves voluntarily chucked out of Realm One."

Linus wasn't convinced. "Are you sure?"

"Almost sure. I found a way of getting into a parallel network linked to the database. The problem is, everything is coded. For the time being, I only know part of the code, but apparently the frontier between realms isn't so watertight."

Linus began to perspire. He rubbed his moist palms against his pants. "So it's possible," he whispered.

"I think so, Cookie. It's just dangerous."

chapter 9

After swiping their ID cards under the camera eye at the station exit, Linus and Chem stopped in front of the Computerized Map Terminal to locate the street where Yosh lived.

"It's only five minutes away," Linus said, leading Chem toward an intersection.

That part of the southern suburbs had barely changed in thirty years. The lackluster four-story buildings—housing designed for a young and active population in the early years of the millennium—had been painted green or pink, but nonetheless still looked shabby. The electric cords of the streetlights were visible, hanging between the buildings like clotheslines. Linus thought the weirdest sights were the open-air parking lots and the heavy car traffic in the streets.

"I thought gasoline-powered cars were banned in residential areas," he said in amazement.

"Only in the Protected Zone," Chem replied. "And please stop ogling the passersby as though they were Martians. It's embarrassing!"

Linus lowered his eyes to the sidewalk. "I just

want to see if people in Realm Two look different from us."

"Well, be more discreet about it."

"Fine, I'll stare down at my feet. Anyhow, they have two arms and two legs, don't they?"

"And two noses!" Chem said with a laugh. "Didn't you notice?"

When they got to Yosh's street, Linus stopped in his tracks.

Chem sighed. "What's wrong? Are you scared?"

Linus nodded. He felt ill at ease in this suburb. Not only were the details different, but the atmosphere was so alien. If Chem hadn't been with him, Linus would have turned back.

"Come on!" Chem said, encouragingly. "We're not going to give up now. Yosh is expecting us."

He grabbed Linus by the sleeve and they made their way into the courtyard of a building. At seven stories high, it was the tallest building in the neighborhood. Dirty cars were parked side by side under the trees. A short distance away, about a dozen kids were playing football on a patch of lawn, their shouts echoing off the walls.

"It's pretty skanky," Chem said, looking up at the building.

Dogs barked from balconies cluttered with old bicycles and stacks of crushed cardboard boxes.

"Are we going in?"

Linus followed Chem into the lobby. He was about to take out his ID card, but Chem told him the buildings were equipped with old-fashioned videophones.

"What's Yosh's full name?" he asked, posting himself in front of the camera.

"Yosh Bresco."

Chem pressed the buzzer for *Bresco*. A voice came on, saying, "I'm letting you in. It's the sixth floor."

When Linus stepped out of the elevator onto the sixth floor, he started shivering. His lower lip trembled. He wondered what he was doing there. The whole expedition suddenly struck him as completely absurd. He and Chem walked slowly along the dark landing. It was not a welcoming place. Broken objects, including a dismantled refrigerator and the carcass of a stroller, were strewn along one wall. In a plastic pot was a plant that had shed most of its leaves.

One of the doors on the landing swung open and Yosh emerged. He stood there, smiling, his hair in spiky tufts.

"Hi, Linus!" he called out. "It's great to finally meet you."

Chem went up to him. "Hi! I think Linus is sick. You'll have to excuse him; he has the jitters."

Linus took a deep breath and went up to Yosh too. "I'm not sick," he protested, smiling with embarrassment. "Chem is a pain. I warned you."

"A pain—that's a new one. You only said 'stubborn as a mule,' " Yosh reminded him with a laugh.

As Yosh moved aside to let his visitors into the apartment, Linus couldn't help smiling to himself. He'd just realized that spelling mistakes couldn't be heard, so orally Yosh was able to fool people completely.

chapter 10

Yosh was odd. He was as tall as Chem but not as muscular. His head was long, and flat on top, like an anvil, with an uneven, chaotic mop of spiky hair on it. When he moved, he seemed clumsy and abrupt—and he almost bumped into the wall every time he went through a door.

There was very little furniture in his house. Yosh claimed that this left more room for humans. After showing Chem and Linus around, he led them to his bedroom. "I'd rather we go there in case my mother comes home."

"I thought your parents worked on Saturday," Linus said, surprised.

"Usually they do, but these days there are a lot of strikes in the Industrial Zone. My mother sometimes comes home without warning because all the roads are blocked by strikers. Haven't you heard about it on the news?"

Chem and Linus shook their heads.

"I'm too dumb to understand what it's all about," Yosh went on, "but I think all hell is going to break loose. I heard my father talking on the phone and that's what he said."

"I was wondering how people manage to work down

there," Linus said. "Do they wear masks in order to put up with the foul odor?"

"Yes, they do," Yosh said. "But my mother claims it isn't very effective. When she comes home from work, she washes her clothes right away, or else they stink up the place. Here in the building, you can immediately tell who works in the I.Z. merely by breathing."

Yosh laughed, then went to the kitchen to get some drinks. Left alone, Chem and Linus looked at each other questioningly.

"He's a nice guy," Chem said. "You were right, he isn't a retard."

Linus agreed and looked pleased. His nervous jitters were gone. He was relaxing. Yosh's house seemed familiar to him, probably because of the photos Yosh had sent him. Sitting on Yosh's bed, he started to play with a little rubber bear. When Yosh returned with some soft drinks, he pointed at the toy. "That's my aunt's latest gift," he said. "Squeeze it!"

Linus squeezed the bear's belly and it started grunting electronically.

"It's for babies," Yosh said.

"You should have thrown the gift in her face," Chem said.

Yosh put the drinks down on his desk. "No, it's good this way. I like my aunt a lot. As long as I don't say much, my parents leave me alone, and no one asks me to do anything. It's good."

Linus gave Yosh a worried look. "Are you sure you

don't want things to change? You could prove to them you're intelligent!"

Yosh ran his hand through his hair as if to comb it, but to no avail; it still stuck up, naturally disheveled. He shrugged and sat down on the floor.

"I'm not intelligent," he announced. "There are things I can't learn. You saw my writing."

Linus threw the bear down on the bed. "Listen, Yosh," he began, "Chem and I have an idea, and I'd like to talk to you about it."

Chem, who was slumped in a chair, sat up. "Hey, wait a minute! First of all, it was your idea. Secondly, I'm not sure . . ."

All of a sudden a deafening noise came from the stairwell, drowning out Chem's voice. It sounded as if a heavy object had tumbled down the steps, exploding in front of the door with a crash of metal and glass.

"What was that?" Chem asked, looking first at Linus, then at Yosh.

"Don't worry." Yosh smiled. "It's only my neighbor. The upstairs one. He's a bit . . . special. He throws things down the stairs sometimes. Now we'll hear yelling."

Sure enough, shouts could be heard through the thin walls of the apartment. Men's and women's voices complained about the "special" neighbor.

"You want to come see?" Yosh asked. "It's quite a show."

He got up and went toward the front door, followed by Chem and Linus.

A crowd had gathered on the landing. Other people were still arriving from the lower floors, shouting, "When the hell will this racket stop? What did he throw out this time?"

"It's a TV!" one woman said as the baby she held in her arms cried.

Several dogs stuck their muzzles out on the landing and began barking. People barked back to make them stop. In the midst of this racket, two men decided to climb to the top floor to beat up the TV thrower.

"This is crazy," Linus whispered.

"It's routine," Yosh replied. "Last week, it was a refrigerator."

"But why does he do this?" Chem asked, totally bewildered.

Shouts and threats were heard from the floor above. Suddenly the two avengers came running down the stairway.

"Quick! Take cover!" one of them yelled. "He's armed!"

Panic broke out on the landing. People jumped over the debris of the broken television and rushed into their apartments, screaming and kicking their dogs to get them back inside. At the top of the stairs, a man appeared, holding a gun.

"Shut the door!" Chem yelled to Yosh.

"Don't panic," Yosh said. "It's a plastic gun." He went out onto the landing.

Frightened, Chem and Linus hid behind the door. "He's completely nuts!" Chem whispered.

Yosh waited by the stairs as the armed man came down toward him. The man was short and pudgy and wore a cap. He was smiling. "So, Yosh!" his voice boomed. "Not a bad trick, the TV, eh?"

Yosh laughed. "A huge racket! I was wondering why you hadn't thrown it down yet."

"It's a choice piece," the man said, putting away his gun. "I didn't think my water pistol would frighten them, though. Too bad no one's here to listen to me."

"I'm here," Yosh pointed out. "And so are my friends." He gestured toward the door of his apartment and called out, "Linus! Chem! You can come out. Let me introduce you to Mr. Zanz."

Chem was clutching the doorknob in distress.

"You coming?" Linus asked him.

Chem rolled his eyes. "They're all nuts in this building. We should bail."

Linus shook his head and went out onto the landing. "Don't mind Chem," he said. "He's got the jitters." Then, without hesitating, he went up to Mr. Zanz.

chapter 11

Mr. Zanz explained his behavior. "By throwing objects down the stairwell, I provoke reactions. People say I'm crazy; they're horrified. But the important thing, for me, is to get them to come out of their apartments. They gather on the landing, complain, and express their opinions. It's the only way to get them talking to one another."

"People here work really hard all day," Yosh said. "In the evening they collapse in front of their TVs and zone out."

"And today," Mr. Zanz added proudly, "for once, the TV collapsed in front of them. I want to show them that things are not unchangeable, roles can be reversed."

Linus looked at him with interest—at his chubby face, small green eyes, and salt-and-pepper hair sticking out from his cap. He had to be in his forties.

"They think I'm crazy." Mr. Zanz laughed. "They may not be wrong. Fortunately, I've got Yosh here." He gave Yosh a friendly tap on the back that made Yosh blush.

"My parents don't like me hanging out with Mr. Zanz," he said to Linus. "They think he's a bad influence on me."

"How about coming upstairs to my place for a few minutes?" Mr. Zanz suggested.

"Sure," Yosh said. "Why not?"

Linus turned to Chem, who had finally let go of the doorknob but was still standing warily at the entrance to Yosh's apartment.

"You coming?" he asked.

Chem wrinkled his nose.

"Suit yourself," Linus said, catching up with Yosh and Mr. Zanz, who'd already started climbing to the seventh floor.

Chem grumbled but followed them, dragging his feet.

Mr. Zanz's apartment looked identical to Yosh's, except for one difference: the walls were lined with books. Linus ran his fingers over the damaged spines. The books were piled up in jumbles, many with dog-eared pages and pieces of paper sticking out from them. This bookcase definitely wasn't a decorative element. It looked as if it was actively used.

"I haven't read all the books," Mr. Zanz explained to Linus. "But I'm happy to lend them out. Yosh often borrows from me. You can help yourself if you want as well."

He vanished into the kitchen and came back a second later, a box of biscuits in his hand. While Linus sat down on the couch, Yosh encouraged Chem to enter the room. "Come on in," he said. "Mr. Zanz is very interested in computer science. I'm sure you could teach him a thing or two."

"Yosh is right. I love computers," Mr. Zanz said. "I've even created a server."

Chem got closer to the couch. "What kind of server?"

Mr. Zanz pretended not to have heard the question. He turned toward Linus, holding out the box of biscuits.

"What about you?" he asked. "Aren't you Yosh's correspondent? He told me about a teenage boy who lives in the north, in the Protected Zone."

"That's me," Linus said, smiling.

"So." Mr. Zanz rubbed his chin. "From what I hear, you're interested in accidents."

Linus winced and glared at Yosh. "You told him?"

"Don't get mad," Mr. Zanz said. "Yosh has no one to talk to here. His parents can't possibly understand the things he has on his mind. So he comes to see me. To get back to accidents—if you're still interested—I too am an accident victim."

Silence descended over the living room. Trying to look natural, Yosh and Mr. Zanz dug into the box for some biscuits. Linus and Chem exchanged quick glances.

"What kind of accident?" Linus asked after the long pause.

Mr. Zanz swallowed his mouthful and leaned against an armchair. His green eyes glimmered with intelligence.

"As it happens, I talk about it a lot on the server I created," he began. "But there's no way you could know about it. It's a completely coded server."

Standing behind the couch, Chem gave a start.

"Aha!" Mr. Zanz laughed. "I see this intrigues our computer genius."

"My name is Chem," Chem said, slightly offended.

"I know. Chem Nogoro. You'll be fourteen on March fourth and you're a student at the Fifth District high school. You're an only child, and you're pretty good at avoiding the Internet security cops, but not good enough to escape me!"

Chem recoiled. Linus too was startled. He didn't know what to do. Run away? Stay? Or have another biscuit?

"Have another biscuit," Mr. Zanz said. He smiled. "As for you, Chem, stop sulking. No one but me knows anything. And you can be sure I wouldn't squeal on you."

"You can trust him," Yosh said. "Mr. Zanz is one of the first people to have succeeded in outwitting the Great Processor."

chapter 12

"This was over twenty years ago," Mr. Zanz was saying. "Children were already required to be tested by the Great Processor, but a number of parents created associations to fight against the unfairness of the system. They denounced the computing methods and the crudeness of the score results. Unfortunately society didn't support them as they might have wished. The majority of parents preferred having the Great Processor decide their children's future. Within a short period of time, insurgent associations were banned. Rising up against the system became illegal."

Mr. Zanz looked at the ceiling as though trying to summon up his recollections. Yosh, Chem, and Linus were sitting around the coffee table and didn't move as they waited for Mr. Zanz to continue his story.

"At fourteen, the legal exam age, I was a bright student, and gifted in computer science, among other things. But I was from a humble background. My parents lived in the Open Zone; they were ordinary Realm Two workers. I knew the Great Processor would give me a Realm One classification. I objected to this sentence. To avoid it, I created a program that would scramble the scores."

"And it worked!" Chem cried out in admiration.

"Yes. It did."

"This is what you call your accident?" Linus asked.

"It is an accident of sorts. At any rate, it's the kind of accident you're interested in, isn't it?"

Linus blushed slightly, but agreed. "I wanted to discuss it with Yosh. That's why we came to see him. I know nothing about life in Realm Two. So before making up my mind, I wanted Yosh to tell me what it's like here."

"Before making up your mind?" Mr. Zanz repeated, puzzled. "Making up your mind about what?"

"About altering it all. You just said the scores can be altered. That's what I want to do."

Yosh got up from the couch, bumped his leg on the corner of the coffee table, and hobbled to the window. Outside, the weather was turning gray.

"Well, you won't be the first ones to take the plunge," Mr. Zanz said. "The coded server Chem discovered recounts the stories of people who have outsmarted the Great Processor. Since Yosh told me about the two of you, I identified Chem and made the connection. Yosh and I immediately figured out your plan. We wanted to see you to decide on the proper procedure."

"So," Linus began, "the TV trick—"

"No," Mr. Zanz interrupted him, "even if you hadn't been here, I would have thrown it down the stairs. But I also thought it was a good way of meeting you."

"Right!" Chem shook his head. "We almost ran off!"

"If you'd left," Yosh said, quietly, "I'd have been

upset. Really upset." He turned from the window and walked over to Linus. "You don't know everything about the exam. The scores can't be altered."

"But Mr. Zanz just said the opposite!" Linus argued.

"I said 'scramble' the scores," Mr. Zanz pointed out. "There's a difference."

Linus felt increasingly uncomfortable, with the unpleasant sensation that the whole thing was beyond him.

"What difference?" he cried out. "I don't understand."

Yosh sat down in front of the coffee table and placed his hands flat on top of it. Slowly he spread out his fingers until his thumbs met, and took a deep breath before continuing. "In order to alter a person's score," he began, "you have to know exactly what the Great Processor computes. And that's precisely what no one knows. The people who have been computed don't remember a thing."

Mr. Zanz sighed. "General amnesia. The Great Processor erases our memories right after the exam. How it does this, I don't know, but that's the only explanation."

"I thought it was a secret. I thought adults didn't speak to us about it to keep it a surprise," Chem said.

Mr. Zanz shook his head. "I suspect that each person must invent a recollection of the exam according to his or her fantasies. Reality completely vanishes. And since the facts about the exam are carefully hidden, I fear they can't be very pretty."

"Since the scores can't be altered," Yosh added impatiently, "the only thing to do is swap. Switch around the scores of two people." He looked at Linus.

A heavy silence fell over the room. It felt as if the heat had been turned up several notches. Linus tried to withstand Yosh's gaze, which was almost painfully insistent.

"A swap?" he said finally, to free himself from the gaze. "Does this mean we would swap identities?"

"No," Yosh said. "Your name would still be Linus Hoppe, but you'd be admitted into Realm Two instead of me. And I would be admitted into Realm One instead of you." He swallowed hard and added, "If we swap scores, do you know what to expect?"

Linus lowered his head and looked at his feet. "What to expect? Living in a building like this and throwing TVs down the stairs, like Mr. Zanz . . ."

Mr. Zanz laughed. "To each his own method," he said. "There are many more renegades than people think. At present, some of my comrades are fomenting strikes in the Industrial Zone. Did Yosh tell you about it?"

Linus suddenly felt his heart pounding too loudly. He started sweating. "I still need to think about it," he mumbled. "It's late. We have to get home."

Yosh crossed the living room. Without turning around, he said, "Me too. I have to think about it too. We'll get back in touch on the WEF."

On the return trip, Chem and Linus hardly exchanged a word. Linus was bewildered. Their incursion into the strange world of Yosh and Mr. Zanz had left a bitter taste in his mouth. The train's vanilla-scented passageways seemed almost pleasant in comparison. When they parted, Chem shook hands with him and asked, "Do you think we'll proceed?"

Linus swayed from one foot to the other, indecisively. "We'll have to see," he said. "I feel like I've been had. Yosh knows much more than we do, and—"

"And you don't want to be manipulated. Neither do I. If you want, we'll stop everything, and each of you will go his own way—you to Realm One, and Yosh to Realm Two. After all, that's where you're supposed to end up."

Linus glanced at his wristwatch. It was late. His parents were probably worried. "Maybe," he said, bringing the conversation to a close. "Why do we absolutely want to change everything, huh?" He smiled at Chem. "See you Monday."

As he took a fork in the passageway, Linus started whistling. He wanted nothing more than to stop thinking about all this, to give his brain a rest, to go back to his quiet, high school student's life, to erase Yosh and Mr. Zanz from his memory, and to act as if nothing had happened. "In fact," he said to himself, "nothing has happened. I'm going to go home, study this week's lessons, and everything will be as usual."

He felt elated as he stepped onto his suburban train. Now he was safe. He merely had to ride without thinking. His watch beeped. It was the e-mail feature. Linus pressed a button and read the message on the tiny screen. *Hurry home, Linus. We're waiting for you to go to Mieg's party! Mom.*

"Darn!" said Linus. "I completely forgot about the party!"

He sent a message back saying he was on his way. Mieg must be furious. The party at the Higher Institute of Architecture meant a great deal to her.

chapter 13

Car traffic was permitted in the Protected Zone under the following conditions:

- the car had to be a nonpolluting vehicle (running on electricity, natural gas, or compressed air);
- it had to carry at least three passengers;
- it had to take the shortest road to the nearest underground highway entrance;
- it had to be used for an emergency or the conveyance of disabled persons.

The Hoppe car stopped by the checkpoint terminal and was given a green light. In the rear, Mieg nervously kicked the bottom of the driver's seat.

"Calm down, Mieg!" Mr. Hoppe ordered. "We set out a bit late, but I promise you we'll get there before the official start of the party."

"A bit late!" Mieg yelled, choking with resentment. "Almost an hour!"

Linus slid closer to his side of the car, to get as far away as possible from his sister's anger. He had run home as soon as he had gotten off the train. His parents had been waiting for him outside, in front of the car. He hadn't even had time to change or apologize or offer an explanation.

Mieg was now on the verge of tears. Mrs. Hoppe was driving calmly, close to the speed limit, without uttering a word.

Though it only accepted Realm One elite, the Higher Institute of Architecture was located in the Open Zone. Mieg often complained about this, as it meant passing through the disreputable sections of the city every day. But the institute board felt that the students benefited by staying in contact with the harsh realities of the unprotected zones during their training. So Linus found himself in the Open Zone for the second time in one day, though the circumstances were very different.

The car emerged from the tunnel and was guided to the parking area by the car computer.

"Hurry!" Mieg said, anxiously.

The Hoppe family took the first parking spot they found, jumped out of the car, ran down the lanes of the underground parking area, found the elevator, dashed inside, dashed out, crossed the street, and finally pushed open the glass door of the building where the party was being held. Mieg took off her coat and ran to join her friends. While Linus unbuttoned his jacket, his parents questioned the hostess. Luckily the opening speech had not yet been given. Linus heaved a sigh of relief. His mother came and hung up her coat on top of his.

"So," she said, "would you mind telling us what you were up to all day?"

"I was with Chem," Linus replied. "We were studying."

"And, of course, you forgot all about the party?"

Linus gave her the look of a submissive dachshund. Mrs. Hoppe responded with a skeptical smile. "Come, let's go listen to the speech and afterward we'll admire Mieg's fresco."

They entered a huge reception room made of metal and wood. It was dotted with pedestals bearing shapes covered with canvas sheets. More than a hundred people were crowded in front of a dais. Linus saw Mieg on the platform, along with ten other students. A pale, lanky, bearded man tested the microphone by tapping it with his fingers, then asked for silence. "Ladies and gentlemen, before I begin I would like to thank you for coming. It is heartening to see so many of you. This party is something we feel very strongly about."

Standing in the crowd, Linus tried to concentrate on the speech. But he couldn't help glancing at the people around him. They were attractive, well dressed, and prosperous looking. He recalled that just two hours before, he'd been in a dingy apartment at the other end of town. *What a contrast!* he thought.

". . . as an occasion for presenting our students' work. The works will be displayed one by one. But first I would like to tell you how proud we are of giving our future architects the opportunity to express themselves through the arts. . . ."

Linus turned around and noticed a gigantic canvas sheet concealing the wall at the far end of the room. Mieg's fresco must be hidden underneath. He looked back at his sister standing on the platform. She looked lovely in her green dress and was happily gazing out at the audience. Her cheeks were flushed, her eyes sparkling. *Compared to her, I look like a pitiful scarecrow,* Linus thought, remembering he hadn't even had time to slip on a shirt. His old black sweater was shapeless and hung loosely over the pockets of his everyday pants.

At the end of the speech, people applauded and spoke in hushed voices among themselves. Then the time came to unveil the works. Each canvas sheet was removed to applause, revealing a misshapen sculpture or assorted objects glued together in a cluster.

"It's Mieg's turn," Mr. Hoppe whispered, taking out his camera.

Linus turned toward the platform. Mieg, greatly excited, waved to him. Apparently she was no longer angry.

The canvas sheet was taken down—and Linus's mouth gaped. Behind him, his parents cried out in astonishment. Mieg's huge fresco showed the Hoppe family sitting at their dining room table, with plates and cutlery in front of them. In the center of the table was the main dish: an enormous book. Linus couldn't take his eyes off the painting. He stared at himself seated at the table, a napkin tied around his neck, a fork in his hand, looking greedy. On his right, his mother sat with her eyes on the big book, and she was rubbing her hands while his father was getting ready to carve the book as though it were a roast chicken. Mieg, her hands flat on the table, serenely awaited her turn. She had painted a title on the cover of the book: *Universal Culture and Knowledge: A Taste for Learning*.

As other works were unveiled, the crowd drifted to different parts of the room. But the Hoppe family stayed rooted in front of the painting portraying them.

"Well?" Mieg asked as she joined them. "How do you like it?"

"It's certainly . . . striking," Mr. Hoppe said, holding his camera in midair.

"Really astonishing," Mrs. Hoppe added.

"I told you you were in for a surprise," Mieg whispered. Then she turned to Linus, awaiting his verdict, but he couldn't think of anything sensible to say. "Why the napkin around my neck?" was all he could mutter. "I'm not a baby anymore."

Mieg rolled her eyes. "You're really incredibly touchy! Do you know how much time it took me to—"

"Please, no quarreling here!" Mrs. Hoppe cut in.

"Come," Mr. Hoppe said to Mieg. "We're going to take some pictures, as promised." He took her by the arm and led her closer to the fresco. Linus stayed with his mother.

"You could try a bit harder," Mrs. Hoppe said. "Or do you enjoy hurting your sister's feelings?"

Linus scowled. "I'm not doing it on purpose. She's overreacting. Anyway, what did she expect? Did she think I'd jump up and down and call her a genius?"

"That's enough. You're really insufferable lately!"

"I just don't like the portrait," Linus said. To avoid further discussion, he walked to the other end of the room and helped himself to the buffet.

chapter 14

"Well?" Chem asked on Monday.

He and Linus were sitting on their favorite bench in the school courtyard. It was a beautiful, mild day. They'd put their coats down, all rolled up, by their sides. The sun tickled their noses.

"Well," Linus replied, "Mieg has been upset at me for two days."

"I don't blame her. After all, you could have praised her fresco even a little."

"No. I thought about it. But do you realize what her painting implies? She's depicted four people from the same family sharing universal culture and knowledge. The idea is so self-centered."

"That might not have been the message she intended."

"Then it's even worse. Her painting is a complete failure."

Chem shook his head. "Sometimes the weirdest things get you all riled up. You're even weirder than I am. Saturday night, when we said goodbye, I thought you wanted to drop the whole thing."

"I did. That visit with Yosh scared me stiff."

"And now you still want to go ahead? All because of

your sister's fresco? You know, Cookie, you're really fickle."

"Fickle? Me?"

"Yes, *you*."

Linus leaned back, laughing. "You're right. I keep changing my mind. But when I saw myself on that fresco, a napkin tied around my neck, ready to gobble up that huge book, it made me nauseous."

"And when you were at Yosh's, you were scared. Is there anyplace you feel well, Cookie?"

Linus turned glum. The trees in the gray courtyard were beginning to bud. There was just a month and a half left before the exam.

"I won't change my mind this time," Linus said, solemnly. "If Yosh agrees, and if Mr. Zanz's network is willing to help us, let's do it."

Chem fidgeted and started swinging his big feet nervously back and forth. "I couldn't resist returning to the coded server," he admitted. "From what they say, once the process is set in motion, you can't go back. It becomes too dangerous and puts their entire system in jeopardy. So if you decide now, that's it; you can't change your mind."

"You know what Mieg's fresco was missing?" Linus asked in response.

"No. Tell me."

"Eight billion dinner guests."

Right after class, without saying goodbye to anyone, Linus rushed to the school's rear exit. What he called the rear exit was a former emergency exit with a metal gate that was easy to climb over. All the students were aware of this shortcut, which led to a boulevard opposite the official exit, but very few dared use it. Linus knew that if he was caught, he'd be summoned to the administrative unit, an experience that would be far from enjoyable.

But that evening, he decided it was worth the risk. He had only an hour and a half to carry out his plans.

When he reached the gate, he slipped his backpack between the bars, jumped, grabbed the top railing, and swung his body over to the other side. He picked up his bag, walked down a narrow concrete passageway, crossed the boulevard, and ran to the entrance of the Zip station without looking back.

Once inside the train, he rested his forehead on the windowpane and caught his breath.

Linus had made up his mind just a short while before, during his introductory finance course. As students concentrated on their exercises of buying and selling on a virtual stock exchange program, Linus too focused on making profitable transactions. He paid no attention to Chem. Suddenly all the screens posted *System Error*. The class erupted in turmoil. Students called out to each other and got up from their desks. The teacher ran from terminal to terminal, sweating, trying out all the keys, unable to do anything about the breakdown. Meanwhile Chem was tipping back his chair and smiling.

"Who disabled the program?" the teacher asked, livid.

Chem stood up without hesitating. "I did."

The teacher was about to shout, but Chem pulled the rug out from under his feet. "You're right, sir," he said, calmly. "It's time I got reeducated in Realm Three." He collected his things and left the classroom. A long silence ensued. Then the teacher launched into a speech: Chem was a teenage rebel, a fool who was ruining his chances, a dangerous individual, an example of what to avoid at all costs.

After his initial astonishment, Linus felt a cold rage well up in him. Not against Chem, but against himself and the school. Chem was right! The course was pointless! That incident clarified Linus's thoughts. And now, riding in the train, he knew exactly what he needed to say to Yosh.

He rushed to the station exit. This time he paid no attention to the dinginess of the buildings, to the passersby, the cars, or the dogs. He knew his way and was no longer afraid.

When he rang the downstairs buzzer, a woman's voice answered. It had to be Yosh's mother! Disconcerted, Linus stammered his name and came up with a muddled, not very credible explanation involving homework. Yosh's mother grumbled something and turned off the videophone. Linus expected the door to the building to be unlocked, but nothing happened.

He stood in the draft, rubbing his hands together to warm them. But he didn't dare buzz Yosh's apartment again. As he looked overhead, he noticed the sky darkening. A storm was brewing.

Just as Linus had worked up the courage to try the buzzer again, the building door opened and Yosh appeared. He was wearing a faded, outgrown T-shirt and slippers with holes in front. He smiled and didn't seem surprised to see Linus. "I'd rather you didn't come upstairs," he said. "There are people at home. Come, we'll find a quiet spot behind the building."

Linus followed Yosh between rows of cars and along a warehouse with broken windowpanes. They went down a few steps and ended up in front of a deserted sandbox. Yosh walked through it, avoiding the dog excrement, and sat down on an old, rusted sprinkler that stood in the middle. Linus sat down next to him.

"This is where I come when I want peace and quiet," Yosh explained.

"But not when it rains, I hope," Linus said, glancing worriedly at the clouds.

"When it rains, I go up to Mr. Zanz's. How's Chem?"

"Glad you asked," Linus said. "Chem is fine. Very well. He understands it all." Linus recounted what had happened in class, then said, "Chem is terrific. He's intelligent, funny, bright. Yet the teachers are obsessed with only one thing—getting rid of him. It's crazy!" He looked at Yosh and added, "Whereas me, I'm the perfect Realm One puppet. A nice boy, meek as a lamb, who swallows everything he's told. Well, those days are over."

Yosh rubbed his hands to warm himself. He smiled. "So you mean you've made up your mind. You want to make the swap?"

Linus nodded. "The people in Realm One don't rebel. They uphold the system and serve it. They have the power and they do everything to keep it. I don't want to play their game anymore. When Mr. Zanz mentioned strikes the other day, I admit it scared me. I'm not accustomed to that sort of chaos. But Mr. Zanz is right. Action must be taken in Realm Two. That's where things can move forward."

Yosh got up and dragged his feet a few steps in the sand. Then he abruptly turned toward Linus. "I never told you about my brother," he said.

Linus opened his eyes wide. "You have a brother?"

"I didn't tell you everything," Yosh continued. "But now I should. It wouldn't be honest if I didn't." He paused, scraping the sand mechanically with his left foot, lost in thought. "I found out about him only a few months ago, by chance. I came upon some old photos in a box. In one of them my mother was holding a baby in her arms. It wasn't me. She ended up admitting that I had a brother."

Linus shuddered and waited for Yosh to go on.

"Can you imagine?" Yosh cried out. "A brother!"

"But . . . how come . . . I mean . . . ," Linus said, confused. "Where is he?"

Yosh spread out his arms and walked in a circle in the sandbox. "He lives in Realm One. With his adopted family. Ever since I found out, it changed everything for me. You understand?"

"It can't be! Your parents kept this a secret?"

Yosh shrugged. "They didn't want to upset me. Like I believe that. Well, they sure succeeded."

Dozens of questions popped into Linus's mind, but he asked only, "Why didn't they keep him?"

"He was born one year after me. You saw our apartment. My parents couldn't afford to bring up two children. They arranged to have him adopted. Or so they said." A pained smile crossed Yosh's lips. "He probably has a good life over there," he muttered, "in Realm One, with wealthy people. A beautiful house, a good education." His voice trembled and he fell silent.

Linus was dumbfounded. "I understand," he said, finally.

"How can you understand?" Yosh said. "You lead a normal life. With normal parents. There are no surprise brothers busting into your life. You can't possibly understand."

"Yes, I can. I can understand that you want to try to find him."

"If I'm admitted into Realm One, I can look for him. If I stay in Realm Two, that won't be possible. So you see, it's important for me to . . ." Yosh's voice cracked and his eyes were moist.

Linus got off the sprinkler and put his hand on Yosh's shoulder.

"Please don't say anything to the others about my brother," Yosh said.

"I won't. It's your secret. I swear."

In the sky, the clouds burst open. The first raindrops

began to fall, making tiny craters in the sand. Linus and Yosh shivered, not knowing whether from cold or fear. Linus tilted his head back and opened his mouth to taste the rainwater. The world seemed to be spinning around him at full speed. He felt dizzy, as if under the spell of an unknown, exciting, intense feeling.

"You'll find him!" he said. "I'm sure of it!"

chapter 15

The following month, using his and Chem's need to study intensively as an excuse, Linus often slept over at Chem's house. No one disturbed them there. Mr. and Mrs. Nogoro, who both worked for health organizations affiliated with other countries, were constantly on the move. The boys stayed connected to Mr. Zanz's server. They learned how to infiltrate databases in real time, as well as how to change names, codes, and file numbers. Chem was very good at this, but if a problem arose, a member of Mr. Zanz's network—a Realm One renegade—was ready to take over operations.

Yosh and Linus had agreed not to see each other until everything was in place. They e-mailed, but avoided alluding to their plan.

When Linus was home, he couldn't seem to hide his moodiness. His parents criticized him for his surly behavior and sudden outbursts. His quarrels with Mieg became unbearable. *All for the better!* Linus thought. *That way I'll have no regrets about leaving!* But each time, he was overcome by a rush of fear and anguish that stuck in his throat. He wondered what had gotten into him. He woke up in the middle of the night with terrifying nightmares. At other moments, he couldn't stop crying. He wanted to crawl into his mother's arms and tell her everything. But that was out of the question. If he broke down, he risked exposing Mr. Zanz's entire organization and endangering the lives of dozens of people. The renegades would be sent to Realm Three, or worse, directly to prison.

One evening, as Linus soaked in the tub, with bubble bath up to his ears, Mieg barged into the bathroom. Without saying a word, she sat on the edge of the tub, arms folded. Linus didn't move and didn't look at her.

"You okay?" Mieg asked.

"Hmmm."

"What does 'hmmm' mean? I'm not asking you to confide in me; I'd just like to put my mind at rest."

"About what?"

"Well, I don't know. You're so irritable lately. I overheard a conversation between Mom and Dad. They're worried seeing you like this."

"Seeing me like what?"

"Like this!" Mieg said, annoyed. She bolted up. "You're acting like you don't understand, but you know very well what I mean."

"No, I don't."

Mieg paced around the bathroom, sighing. She stopped in front of the mirror. "Do you think I look fat?" she asked.

"I don't know."

"I've put on eleven pounds this winter. I'm becoming

huge. And I have pimples and . . ." She hesitated. "And I'm fed up," she muttered.

Linus sat up in the foamy water and looked at her. "I don't think you're fat," he said.

Without looking away from her reflection, Mieg blurted, "You don't want to do well on the exam, am I right?"

Linus felt his heart pounding in his chest. He stifled a cry of protest and waited to hear what his sister would say next.

"I figured it out," Mieg continued. "You're constantly criticizing the system. Maybe you think you don't belong in Realm One, but you're wrong."

Linus played dumb. "What makes you think that?"

Mieg approached the bathtub again. "Just a feeling I have," she said. "But I suppose you don't want to discuss it with me."

"I have nothing to say."

Before leaving the bathroom, Mieg ran her fingers through her hair. Her dark curls fell back over her eyes.

"You and Chem are about to make a huge, stupid mistake," she said. Then she promptly stomped out of the bathroom.

Linus was in shock. How had Mieg guessed? What exactly did she know? He was mad at himself for not having been more careful. With her habit of prying into everything, Mieg might have surfed the WEF and discovered something.

Linus got out of the tub, dried himself off, and

quickly got dressed. Questions were whirling in his head—alarming questions. If the Internet was unsafe, the telephone was even more so. Only one solution remained: he had to go out. He had to warn Chem, Yosh, and Mr. Zanz. That night! Linus went back to his room, slipped on his shoes, and tiptoed down to the foyer. His parents would be home any minute, so he needed to leave right away. Mieg hadn't heard him. She was in her room, no doubt working. The coast was clear. He scribbled a few words on a piece of paper.

I'm at Chem's. I'll be home late. Don't worry about me.

Linus

After putting the note in a conspicuous place, he opened the front door. The night-light in the hallway turned red. He hoped Mieg wouldn't notice. Linus made his way outside and along the path noiselessly. The gate squeaked slightly when he opened it. His heart pounding, he raced down the street to the Zip.

Inside, the crowd wasn't as dense as during rush hour. Linus edged his way between people, afraid of meeting someone he knew. When he got to the platform, he caught his breath. Luckily a train pulled in immediately, and Linus took a seat on the lower level.

Twenty minutes later, the train came to its first stop in Paris. Linus was supposed to get off at the following stop, but the train wasn't budging. The ticket inspector's voice crackled over the loudspeaker with an announcement: "Ladies and gentlemen, a demonstration is taking place in the station. The train is being held up. We request that you disembark and make your way to the exits or transfer to connecting service."

Linus put his head in his hands as travelers started getting off the train, complaining loudly. It was already 8:45 p.m. When he joined the others on the platform, he noticed a gathering of about fifty men and women. A few were on the track, in front of the train. Others were on the platform, blocking the exits. They were brandishing banners inscribed with slogans: *Workers and Employees of the I.Z., Join the Strike!* and *Say No to Mind-Numbing Work!*

Linus remembered Mr. Zanz's remarks. There had to be some renegades among the strikers. Without further thought, Linus made his way toward the group. Shouts and chants rang out while some demonstrators jostled the Trans-Urban agents who were trying to break up the demonstration. Linus spotted Mr. Zanz in the middle of the crush. "Mr. Zanz!" he cried out, waving his arms.

In the confusion, no one heard him. So Linus elbowed his way into the group. Mr. Zanz was right in front of him, busily yelling out orders. Linus tugged at his sleeve and Mr. Zanz turned around, annoyed.

"Mr. Zanz! Excuse me for disturbing you, but I—"

"What are you doing here?"

"I have to talk to you! Something's happened!"

Mr. Zanz was swept away to the edge of the track by a

movement in the crowd. Linus barely managed to squeeze himself between a burly guy bellowing insults and a red-faced woman holding up a banner. These people looked angry. Standing on tiptoes, Linus saw Mr. Zanz dragging the train conductor out of his booth. The Trans-Urban agents were being pushed back without any consideration. Linus tried to get nearer, but just as he reached Mr. Zanz, they heard a stampede, the blowing of whistles, and shouts. Mr. Zanz froze on the spot. "Withdraw!" he cried out. "Stop everything! They're going to corner us!"

The group of demonstrators broke up in sudden panic. Terrified, Linus clung to Mr. Zanz as best he could.

"You're still here!" Mr. Zanz yelled at him. "You don't realize what you're getting into."

He grabbed Linus by the hand and pulled him away. Linus raced down the passageways along with the others. The underground police were hot on their heels. Cries reverberated; travelers were shoved. His stomach churning, Linus kept a firm grip on Mr. Zanz's hand. The group dispersed in the various passageways.

"Hurry!" Mr. Zanz whispered, pushing Linus into a service stairway off-limits to the public.

"But we're not allowed in there!" Linus cried as he stepped back.

"Don't argue!" Mr. Zanz ordered.

Mr. Zanz shut the door behind them. Inside, it was dark, with only a few weak lights dotting the wall down the stairs. Mr. Zanz dragged Linus along steps that plunged into the station's lower depths. They arrived in front of another door, breathless. It was locked. Mr. Zanz reached into his jacket pocket, withdrew a passkey, and opened the door.

They walked down a long concrete passageway. A sickening odor of putrefaction and gasoline made Linus gag. He pulled his scarf over his nose. Mr. Zanz walked ahead of him, tense and silent. Thanks to the key, they went through several doors before reaching a huge warehouse with pipes all over the walls. Linus saw a glass-enclosed office, all lit up, at the far end.

"We're safe here," Mr. Zanz told him. "This is the warehouse of a former construction site, dating back to when the Industrial Zone was built. It's one of my organization's hiding places. Keep that to yourself, of course."

Linus was sweating profusely. He was overcome with dreadful nausea and leaned against the wall only a moment before he threw up.

chapter 16

Ten minutes later, Linus sat in the office, looking pale as a sheet, but feeling slightly better. He took off his jacket and hung it on the back of the chair.

"Was this your first demonstration?" Mr. Zanz asked him, trying to smile.

Linus nodded.

"Well, for a trial run you did all right. The most important thing for a demonstrator is being able to run fast!" Mr. Zanz's expression suddenly turned serious again and he glanced at his wristwatch. "The others are going to join us. You shouldn't have involved yourself in all this. It's very dangerous for young people."

"I wanted to talk to you," Linus said. "Concerning our arrangement. It's my sister. . . . I think she found out about it."

Mr. Zanz frowned. He took off his cap and glasses and put them on the table in front of him. "Explain that to me."

"She hinted. She said Chem and I were about to make a huge, stupid mistake. But, I swear, I didn't say a thing to anyone. Maybe she fiddled with my computer and found something. She's a snoop, you know."

Mr. Zanz got up from his chair and paced the room.

Linus watched him. The office wasn't big. Leaflets had been tacked onto the walls.

"Do you think she could endanger our organization?" Mr. Zanz asked.

"I have no idea. She's my sister. I like her, but she wouldn't understand."

Just then, footfalls echoed in the warehouse. Mr. Zanz gave a start and looked annoyed. Three men and two women burst into the office. They were red-faced, out of breath, and agitated.

"Hey, Zanz! What's with the kid?" one of the women yelled.

"He happened to be in the station. I know him; he won't talk."

The newcomers took off their coats and sat down around the table. One of them started to make coffee, using an antique espresso machine on a corner of the table.

"It almost turned nasty," a man with a southern accent noted. "But everything turned out okay. The others went home."

"Let's put it off till tomorrow," a young woman with short dark hair said as she folded her banner.

Linus listened to the conversation, but the knowledge that he was hundreds of feet underground and far from home made him feel completely lost. A lump rose in his throat and he tried hard not to betray any discomfort.

Mr. Zanz put a hand on his shoulder. "I think you've had enough for one night. I'm taking you home. Wait for me outside the office. I won't be long."

Linus obeyed and Mr. Zanz shut the glass door behind him.

The smell and heat in the warehouse were unbearable. In a corner, construction equipment was stored under canvas covers. *Maybe Yosh's parents work in a place like this,* Linus thought. He turned to look at the office again. Through the glass, he saw Mr. Zanz talking to the young woman and the man with the southern accent. By now, Linus was exhausted and all he wanted was to climb into bed.

Finally Mr. Zanz joined him. They were about to leave the warehouse when the young woman hurried to catch up to them. She was holding Linus's jacket.

"You left it on the back of the chair," she told him. "See you soon, maybe."

Linus took his jacket, and Mr. Zanz led him away. "Come. We'll take the elevator up to the ground floor."

In the elevator, Linus looked closely at Mr. Zanz. Without his glasses, the pudgy man seemed younger. He also looked very preoccupied.

"I didn't tell my colleagues about your problem," he said. "But if your sister found out about us, I have to make sure she hasn't informed against us."

"I'm sure she hasn't." Linus tried to reassure him.

Mr. Zanz was solemn. "Maybe. But I've got to check it out."

Linus began to worry. He didn't appreciate Mr. Zanz's tone of voice. And he was mad at himself for getting embroiled in this mess.

"What are you going to do?" he asked.

"Question your sister. That's the only thing to do. If the others find out there are leaks, there'll only be big trouble."

"But I tell you—"

Mr. Zanz put up a hand. "Now that you're in our files and you know about this hiding place, you almost belong to the organization. This isn't a game, Linus."

As the elevator reached the ground floor, Linus's legs went weak. He felt faint.

"Listen, Linus," Mr. Zanz said. "I know you're afraid, but it's too late to back down. I won't harm your sister, I promise. Let me take you home now."

• • •

By the time they got off the train, it was past eleven o'clock. Mr. Zanz wasn't accredited to enter the Protected Zone, so he left Linus near the gate.

"Please," Linus begged him once more, "leave my sister alone!"

Mr. Zanz scratched his head. Dark circles were forming under his eyes from fatigue. "There is an alternative," he said. "*You* could be in charge of questioning her."

Linus immediately agreed.

"Fine. I trust you," Mr. Zanz said. "But you've got to be honest with me. If you see she wants to turn us in, you have to let me know. Otherwise . . ."

Linus swallowed hard, torn between relief and anxiety.

"Otherwise, you'll pay the consequences. The organization would find it hard to forgive you."

"Okay," Linus agreed, his throat tightening.

"I'll give you forty-eight hours. Contact me again on the server, at this address." Mr. Zanz handed Linus a visiting card. "Get the code from your buddy Chem. If I don't hear from you, I'll take action myself."

Linus nodded and proceeded through the gate. He ran home. The closer he got, the more he appreciated what the term *Protected Zone* meant.

• • •

As soon as he stepped into his house, Linus headed straight up to his room without explaining anything to his parents. He collapsed on his bed, feeling as if his head were about to burst. Suddenly his father opened the door to his room. He looked furious.

"Do you think you can just walk into the house like this, Linus?" he asked, fiercely. "Your attitude is deplorable. Unacceptable! You disappear, then you reappear. And not one word of apology or explanation!"

Linus turned toward the wall.

"Look at me!" his father shouted. "Until proven otherwise, you're still a minor and we have a right to know what's going on. We phoned Chem. You weren't there!"

Linus clenched his teeth. Even if he had wanted to, he couldn't have admitted the truth. Thankfully his father had stopped speaking, but he was sniffing the air in the room.

"What's this odor?" he asked. "It smells like . . . gasoline or . . . Really, Linus, where have you been hanging out?"

Then Mrs. Hoppe walked into the room, sparing Linus from telling another lie.

"Linus," she said. "You've got to understand. We're very concerned about you. I called the headmistress of your school today. Your grades have been getting noticeably lower. Why didn't you tell us? We can help you."

"No!" Linus wailed. "You can't help me! And if, on top of everything, you bawl me out, it'll be worse!"

"So what should we do, then?" his father asked. "Stand by and watch you sink deeper into your problems? You're still only a child!"

"Oh, I am, am I?" Linus laughed nervously. "Then why do I have to take this stupid exam if I'm not old enough to make decisions?"

"That's exactly why!" his father retorted. "The Great Processor spares you from making decisions. And in your case, that's surely for the best!"

Mr. Hoppe walked out of the room, fuming. Mrs. Hoppe was distraught too, but she stayed, looking helpless. Linus breathed deeply a few times to calm himself. The situation was getting impossible for him to deal with. On one hand, he faced his parents' anger; on the other, he faced Mr. Zanz's threats. It was too much!

He started to cry. His mother came over and took him in her arms. At first, she recoiled slightly, no doubt because of the odor in Linus's clothes, but then she acted as if there were nothing unusual.

"You don't have to tell me anything," she whispered. "Cry. It will make you feel better."

While sobbing in his mother's arms, Linus had the unpleasant feeling of playing yo-yo with his life, of flipping up and down between two extreme states. Flip up: he was almost an adult and involved in a demonstration. Flip down: he was a lost boy who needed to be comforted. He wished he could stop somewhere in the middle, but that wasn't possible for a yo-yo.

Gradually he calmed down.

"You're sure you don't want to tell me about it?" his mother asked gently.

Linus shook his head. "Where's Mieg?"

"She must be asleep. You should be too."

"I'll talk to her tomorrow, then," Linus mumbled as his mother got up to leave. And as she turned out the light, Linus drifted off to sleep.

chapter 17

"Did you sleep in your clothes or what?" Mieg said when she saw Linus enter the kitchen the next morning.

"Just about."

Mieg raised her eyebrows. She was busy blending fruits—kiwi, mango, kumquat, citron, blueberry—with mixed exotic nuts, carob, and a lot of yogurt.

"Do you want some?" she asked, watching Linus yawn.

He smiled. "I'll take a double dose."

They sat opposite each other, savoring the mixture ceremoniously. Mr. and Mrs. Hoppe were still upstairs. The fog in Linus's mind gradually cleared, and the events of the past night loomed up with dreadful clarity. There was no time to lose. He had to speak to Mieg.

"You know, I don't find you fat at all," he said, trying to put his sister at ease. "That was silly what you said yesterday."

"That was only because I wanted to talk to you," Mieg admitted. "Though it's true I've put on eleven pounds."

"What did you want to talk to me about? My grades?"

Mieg lowered her eyes and fiddled with the glass between her fingers.

"I heard the conversation Mom had with your headmistress."

"You're always all ears," Linus said. "Why did you say Chem and I were making a huge, stupid mistake? Did you snoop around my room?"

Mieg got up and went to the sink.

"Answer me! Did you snoop?"

"No," Mieg said, turning around.

Linus believed her.

Mieg sat down at the table again. "The day before yesterday, a guy came up to me as I was leaving the institute after class. I didn't know him, but he introduced himself as one of your friends. He looked pretty unusual. His hairstyle, for one . . . well, it was unique."

Linus felt himself go pale. "Yosh," he muttered.

"Yosh, that's it. We talked for quite a while, even though it was windy and chilly. But his story was so astonishing, I was glued to the spot, if you see what I mean."

"You mean Yosh told you everything?" Linus shrieked. "He's completely nuts!"

This piece of news was hard to take. Try as he might, Linus had trouble believing Yosh would do anything so foolish. In fact, it wasn't foolishness; it was sabotage. Linus banged his fist on the table.

Mieg winced. "Calm down! Mom and Dad will hear you!"

"I don't care!" Linus shouted. "The whole thing is hopeless now!"

"Let me finish," Mieg pleaded, lowering her voice. "Yosh explained to me how the two of you met. And, more importantly, what your plans are. At first, I refused to believe him. It seemed crazy to me. But the more he spoke, the more I realized he was telling the truth. You can't imagine what a shock I got!"

"Yosh is a traitor!" Linus said, furious. "He's—he's scum."

"Yesterday, that was all I could think about," Mieg continued. "Last night, I couldn't keep quiet anymore. Especially when I heard you were getting low grades. I realized all the pieces of the puzzle fit together. Your bad moods, your weird questions, your secrets. I've tried talking to you, but you tune me out."

"Why did Yosh do it?"

"Because he got cold feet."

"What about me? Don't you think I've got cold feet?"

Mieg pursed her lips and looked at her brother sadly. "Yosh is very lonely," she said. "He has no one to talk to, and—"

"That's not true! There's more to it than he's saying."

"That's just it! He came to see me so I would warn you about Mr. Zanz."

Flabbergasted, Linus felt his jaw drop open. "You know Mr. Zanz?"

"As I said, Yosh told me everything. There's something

fishy about Mr. Zanz. It's because of him Yosh started to get scared."

Mieg fell silent. She'd just heard their father coming down the stairs, whistling quietly. She drank the last of her shake while Linus stuck his nose into his own glass.

"Well, good morning," Mr. Hoppe greeted them as he walked in. "I see you're both sulking." He stopped near Linus and squeezed his shoulder. "I apologize for losing my temper last night," he said. "It wasn't the best way of helping you. I thought about it, and wondered if all four of us shouldn't go away on vacation for a few days. What do you think?"

Linus and Mieg exchanged worried looks.

"Five days in Florida!" Mr. Hoppe announced, smiling from ear to ear. "How long has Grandma been badgering us to come and see her? She'll be thrilled."

"I can't possibly go," Mieg replied. "I have too much work."

"Me too!" Linus chimed in. "If I want my grades to improve, I have to work hard. The exam is only two weeks away."

"Linus is right," Mieg agreed. "In fact, I'm going to help him prepare for the exam. Right, Linus?"

Linus frowned. "Uh . . . yeah. Mieg made the offer and . . ."

Mr. Hoppe pulled out a chair and dropped into it. "Obviously I don't understand a thing about children." He sighed. "I thought you would jump for joy."

"It's a good idea," Mieg said, soothingly. "But frankly, it's bad timing."

"Very bad timing!" Linus affirmed.

"Okay," Mr. Hoppe said. "I'm going to make myself some very strong coffee."

Mieg looked at the clock. "Oh, gosh, I'd better get moving. You coming, Linus?"

Leaving their father totally baffled, they both headed upstairs to their rooms.

"He doesn't have a clue!" Mieg said.

"No, he doesn't." Linus was relieved. Then he grabbed his sister by the sleeve. "Is it true that you want to help me?"

"Of course." Mieg smiled. "You're my favorite little brother; don't ever forget it."

"You won't inform against us, then?"

"Do you think I'm a dope or something?"

"No. I'm sorry. I was afraid you wouldn't understand."

"I don't," Mieg said. "But that won't prevent me from helping you. I'll tell you what I know about Mr. Zanz on the train, all right? Go change. You look like you haven't washed in a week."

chapter 18

When Linus arrived at school, he tracked down Chem and led him to a quiet corner in the corridor.

"Are your parents around these days?" he asked.

"No." Chem sighed. "They're in Angola."

"Perfect! We need to have a meeting at your place."

"Okay, Cookie, you need to calm down."

"There's no reason to calm down. You'll understand this evening. If I can reach Yosh, there'll be four of us."

"I thought you weren't supposed to see each other before D-day," Chem said, surprised. "Anyhow, that makes three. If you can't count on your fingers, why bother to switch the exam scores?"

"Stop joking!" Linus pleaded. "I'm telling you, something serious has come up. The fourth person is Mieg."

"Your sister? Well, now I'm completely stumped."

"I can't fill you in now. Just trust me. Let's meet at your place at six p.m."

• • •

At 6:05, Linus and Mieg arrived at Chem's house.

"Is Yosh here yet?" Linus asked.

"No," Chem answered.

Chem's apartment was spacious and comfortable. The living room walls were decorated with African masks, Oriental rugs, and musical instruments.

"Gee, this is a real museum," Mieg said as she took a look around.

"My parents brought all these things back from their trips."

"I'll bet you don't see them very often."

Linus let them chat and went to the kitchen window to stand watch. He could see the street and the sidewalk. He hoped Yosh had found a way of getting there.

• • •

Linus had thought the day would never end. Class after class, Chem had made insolent remarks that had infuriated the teachers. "I can't wait for the system to exclude you, Mr. Nogoro!" they'd each told Chem. The students, on the other hand, had one sentence on their lips: "Only two weeks left!" Two weeks! Linus couldn't concentrate. He kept recalling Mieg's words about making a huge, stupid mistake, and each time, they made his heart skip a beat.

Yosh's silhouette appeared at the end of the street. Linus was relieved. He saw that Yosh looked nervous as he crossed over. He kept turning around. Finally he stopped at the door of the building.

"Yosh is here," Linus cried out. "I'm going down to let him in. He isn't accredited for entry."

Linus raced out of the apartment and down the stairway. When he reached the ground floor, he pulled open the heavy glass door. Yosh half smiled at him, then glanced behind himself again before plunging into the lobby. "All clear," he said. "No one followed me."

Linus walked ahead and they went up to Chem's apartment.

"Did you have any trouble entering the city?" Linus asked him.

"I said I had an appointment with my psychologist. The security guards checked to see if I had permission to visit her and they let me through. But this will only work once. I'm sure she'll inform on me."

"When I think about it, it's completely outrageous!" Linus said. "Those of us who live in Realm One have the freedom to go anywhere with our swipe cards, whereas you can't."

They entered the Nogoro apartment and joined Chem and Mieg in the living room. After they'd all made themselves comfortable on the couch, Linus started speaking. "We have convened as an emergency committee," he announced. "Yosh contacted Mieg and filled her in on the secret."

"I'd like to know why," Chem said.

Yosh turned to him. "I couldn't come to see you. I'm being watched and you are too. Linus had told me about his sister and I'd seen her photo. Since her school's in the Open Zone, it was easier for me to go there. I felt I could trust Mieg. Was I wrong?"

"No, Yosh. That was the only thing to do," Linus said, encouraging him. "Tell us what happened. Then I'll tell you about my experience last night."

Chem, wide-eyed, stared at Linus, then looked back and forth between Yosh and Mieg, incredulously.

"Mr. Zanz is betraying us," Yosh began. He took a deep breath before continuing. "Two days ago, I heard noise in the stairwell. Voices, people yelling at each other. I thought Mr. Zanz had chucked something down the stairs again, so I went out to look. But that wasn't it. Three men and two women I'd never seen before were on the landing. When they saw me, they stopped talking and went up to the seventh floor. I didn't worry about it, and shut my door. Later, I heard noise at Mr. Zanz's. My building is the opposite of soundproof. You can even hear the neighbors in their showers. All hell was breaking loose up there. I was afraid Mr. Zanz might be in trouble—maybe even because of us—so I tiptoed upstairs. I heard part of the conversation through the door and it gave me the creeps." Yosh paused to collect his thoughts. The others waited impatiently.

"A woman was saying, 'We need them now!'" Yosh went on. "Mr. Zanz said, 'It's too early! I'll hand them over to you when they can be caught red-handed!' Then I heard a man's voice: 'It's too risky! They could get suspicious!' And Mr. Zanz replied, 'They don't suspect a thing. They trust me completely. One of them even considers me a surrogate father!'" Yosh's voice began to tremble. "Mr. Zanz has completely manipulated me," he said, blowing up. "He wasn't honest. And to think I told him everything!"

"Maybe he was talking about someone else," Linus suggested.

"No. He was talking about us," Yosh insisted. "Later he said, 'Trust me. Don't forget, two of them live in the Protected Zone. They're not easy to trap.' At that point, I got scared and went back downstairs."

Yosh's face turned red and tense. He stood up and started stamping his feet. "It makes me sad," he cried out. "Really sad."

Mieg got up and tried to grasp his shoulders, but Yosh shook off her hands.

"None of you can understand!" he wailed.

Linus was alarmed. He remembered his initial conversations with Yosh on the WEF, when Yosh had told him about his devastating temper tantrums. He hoped Yosh wasn't about to start throwing things out the window. The neighbors would instantly call the police.

"Please calm down," Linus said. "This is the worst possible time for a tantrum. Think of your lion tamer's whip, Yosh."

Yosh started walking around the living room, groaning and howling. He wrung his hands, and convulsions seemed to shake his whole body.

"What can we do to help him?" Mieg asked, alarmed.

"We just have to wait till it's over," Linus replied. "Yosh told me he was starting to master these tantrums. Let's just wait it out."

Yosh folded his arms in an attempt to control his uncoordinated movements. He shut his eyes and uttered some incomprehensible words. Little by little, these sounds seemed to comfort him. He crouched down, wrapped his arms around his legs, and lowered his shoulders and head. He started crying. "I'll be okay," he said, hiccupping. "It's just a small tantrum."

Mieg sat down next to him and put her hand on his back. This time, Yosh didn't push her away. A deep silence settled in the room, broken by Yosh's sobs. Mieg managed to lead him back to the couch, where he curled into a ball.

"One thing bothers me," Mieg said. "You say your building is the opposite of soundproof, Yosh. Mr. Zanz must be aware of this. He should have realized you might overhear his conversation. How do you explain that?"

Yosh shrugged. "Who knows? Maybe he didn't stop to think."

"That seems odd," Mieg insisted. "Someone as organized as Mr. Zanz wouldn't be so reckless."

Linus spoke up. "He probably wasn't warned that the others were coming to see him. He was taken by surprise. From what Yosh heard, these people plan to arrest us. It sounds like they wanted to do it right then and there. Except Mr. Zanz is their leader, so they wanted to discuss it with him first. I think that's why they were arguing on your landing."

"That's possible," Yosh said. "None of this occurred to me."

"But it doesn't make sense," Chem said. "Mr. Zanz gave me the key to a Web site that compiles the statements of dozens of people who have followed the same procedure, and—"

"There's only one explanation for that," Linus cut in. "It's a bogus Web site. Like everything else. Mr. Zanz tricked us into thinking he would help us, but in fact he belongs to some sort of group that intercepts people who want to outwit the Great Processor. Seems obvious to me."

A deathly silence descended over the living room. Outside, night was just beginning to fall. Spring had come to the city; the streets were joyful and bustling, and yet deep down Linus felt a wintry chill. Yosh huddled in a corner of the couch. His strange, flat head gave him a sad, moonfaced look. Chem's leg started trembling nervously. As for Mieg, she sat motionless as a statue.

"I'm sure we're not the first people this is happening to," Linus said. "They're organized. That can't be done overnight. There must be others who've slipped through their net! Real renegades! They might be able to help us!"

Yosh wasn't sure. "Mr. Zanz and his clique are too powerful for us," he said. "Even if we stopped everything now, they'd still keep a close watch on us. With the evidence Mr. Zanz has collected, all three of us will wind up in Realm Three . . . or in prison."

"But we're not crazy or criminal!" Chem shouted. "They have no right!"

"Yes, they do," Linus said. "Trying to outwit the

Great Processor is illegal. My father has explained this to me over and over again: the entire social structure is based on the realm system. The Great Processor is the main link, since it assigns people to the different realms. Yosh is right: we're outlaws."

"You, maybe," Mieg said suddenly, regaining a bit of hope. "But I'm not! I was admitted into Realm One and I'm not being watched. I can help you."

Linus felt himself blush to the roots of his hair. "Well, that's—that's just it," he stammered. "I had something else to tell you."

"What now?" Chem asked, completely dazed by all the revelations.

"I saw Mr. Zanz last night," Linus confessed. As he described his incursion into the underground urban areas in Mr. Zanz's company, he saw his friends go through a range of overpowering emotions. "I'm supposed to get in touch with him again tomorrow evening," Linus added. "I'm supposed to tell him whether Mieg is a danger to his organization. But even if I lie, he'll start watching her too."

Mieg sighed. "It's all my fault! I should have spoken to you right away. Now we're completely cornered."

Chem got up from the couch. With his tall, strong physique, his uncommunicative face, and his clenched fists, he looked like a boxer about to fight his last round.

"There's only one solution left for us," he announced. "We have to short-circuit both Mr. Zanz and the Great Processor at the same time. Meanwhile, we'll have to soothe the suspicions of the people spying on us. Mr. Zanz can't suspect anything. If he does, he'll have us arrested before we can act. We have two weeks to succeed. Do you follow me?"

"Yes," Linus said immediately.

"Same here," said Yosh.

Mieg stayed silent for a moment, staring into space. Then she said, "Count me in."

chapter 19

D-DAY MINUS 13

As Linus typed Mr. Zanz's e-mail address on his computer keyboard, a cold sweat trickled down his back.

"Here's the decrypted code," Chem said.

Linus took the sheet of paper with its chart of seemingly haphazard numbers and letters. "Are you sure you've deciphered it accurately?"

"Absolutely, Cookie. Go ahead and type!"

Linus sent a coded message:

I've questioned my sister. She knows nothing. If you want to check for yourself, go meet her outside the Higher Institute of Architecture this evening at 5:00.

"There." Linus leaned against the back of his chair. "That's done."

Chem nodded. "It's up to Mieg now."

• • •

Mieg was particularly tense that evening as she left the HIA. Yosh had described Mr. Zanz to her. Discreetly she searched the crowd of students, looking for a pudgy man wearing a cap and eyeglasses. No one matched that description. She was about to continue on her way when a young woman approached her.

"Are you Mieg Hoppe?" the woman asked. "Can I speak to you for a few minutes?"

"Who are you?"

"My name won't mean a thing to you. I know your brother, Linus."

"Oh?"

"Please return this to him." She handed Mieg a swipe card. "He lost it, and I found it."

Mieg took the card. It was Linus's pass to the high school multimedia library.

"I'll make sure he gets it. Thank you." Mieg was about to walk off, but the young woman held her back.

"Also, tell your brother he'd better study hard for his exam."

Mieg flinched. "He's studying," she said. "Linus is an outstanding student."

"Is that so? Haven't you noticed a change in him recently?"

"Yes, I have. He's a bit tired. But he's very eager to succeed. I don't see why you're worried about him."

"Fine," the young woman said. "Just tell him not to spend too much time playing around on the WEF. It could distract him."

Mieg frowned and gathered her hair under her hat. "I don't pry into Linus's affairs," she retorted. "Now, excuse me. I have to get home."

Quickly Mieg walked off, leaving the woman standing

alone on the sidewalk. After several dozen yards, Mieg looked back. The woman was still right where she'd left her. Mieg wanted to run, but forced herself to walk at a normal pace. That woman's eyes bored into her back like a warning. Who was she? Could she be one of the people Yosh had seen on the landing?

Mieg was relieved to arrive at the Zip concourse. But just as she reached for her ID card, a hand clamped down on her shoulder. She let out a scream. In front of her was a pudgy man with a cap pulled down tight on his head.

"Are you Mieg Hoppe?" he asked in a low voice.

Mieg nodded, struck dumb. Mr. Zanz's green eyes rolled around wildly like two marbles. He was sweating at the temples.

"I must speak to you."

"But . . . I . . . ," Mieg stuttered. "A woman just stopped me."

"A woman? Did she question you? What did she look like?"

"Uh . . . she was young, with short hair."

"Did she talk about Linus?"

"Yes."

Mr. Zanz wiped the beads of sweat off his forehead.

"We can't stay here," he said. "Let's go into the station."

He pulled Mieg by the arm and led her to the ID terminal. Once inside, Mieg tried to extricate herself from his grasp.

"Stay put!" Mr. Zanz ordered her, tightening his grip. "Something very serious is happening. Linus, Chem, and Yosh are in danger."

Mieg felt her brain getting muddled. She couldn't process this news. Everything was becoming confused. Mr. Zanz pushed her into a corner, sheltered from people's gazes.

"I know your brother well," he said. "My name is Zanz. Did Linus mention me to you?"

"No," Mieg lied, her voice trembling slightly.

"Did he ever tell you about Yosh?"

"Yosh? Never heard of him."

Mr. Zanz sighed. "You probably won't understand a thing I say, but I have no choice. Especially now that that woman got to you first. I'm a stupid fool for not realizing they would read the message before I did. Listen, let me give you something for Linus."

Mr. Zanz took out a piece of paper and a pen. He jotted down a succession of numbers and letters, then slipped the paper into Mieg's hand. "Can I trust you?"

"Yes."

"Then go on, hurry. Linus must get this message as quickly as possible."

Mieg stuffed the piece of paper into her jeans pocket and rushed to the platform, as far away as possible from Mr. Zanz and the crazy look in his eyes.

• • •

They were supposed to meet at Chem's house. The Nogoro apartment had become their group's headquarters. Mieg rushed over there.

"So?" Chem and Linus asked at once.

Mieg caught her breath and briefly told them what had happened. Then she handed her brother his ID card and delivered Mr. Zanz's message.

"Let me see!" Chem cried out. He started decoding the message: *Don't contact me at the address you have. Spies at work. My network infiltrated by police. Danger of being discovered. Yosh informed. See you tomorrow, 8 p.m., in front of your school.*

"What's he up to?" Linus said. "I don't understand anything anymore."

Chem crumpled the paper and threw it on the floor. "We shouldn't trust him. He's a traitor."

"He looked sincere," Mieg said. "He looked truly worried for you. To be honest, I'd say it's the woman who didn't look trustworthy. How did she ever get hold of your library card?"

"It must have fallen out of my jacket pocket the night I went down to their hideout. I definitely remember a woman with short hair among the demonstrators. I forgot my jacket and she's the one who brought it to me."

Chem took the card from Linus's hands and looked it over.

"A person going out of her way to return this piece of plastic to you seems strange."

He went to the computer and swiped the card

through the scanner. At first the machine failed to read it, but Chem didn't give up, and after several more tries, he managed to get it decoded. Numbers popped up on the screen. Chem looked on in silence.

"I don't see anything abnormal," he conceded with disappointment. "This whole story is making me completely paranoid."

Linus took his card back and slipped it into his wallet. "The woman used it to get Mieg to trust her, that's all."

"And what about the meeting with Mr. Zanz?" Mieg asked.

"I'll go," Linus said. "If he comes with Yosh, I have to be there. You and Chem can stay posted nearby. If something suspicious occurs, send me a warning message on my wristwatch."

• • •

D-DAY MINUS 12

The high school gate had been shut for hours. It was night. Linus waited in a dark blind alley, surrounded by almost complete silence. Checking his watch, he read Chem's message: *All clear here.* Then Mieg's message flashed by: *Zanz and Yosh on the corner, coming up the hill!*

Linus watched the entrance to the alley. If anything went wrong, he would have to climb over the gate, jump, run, and pray no one would nab him at the rear exit. It would be risky, but Linus had the advantage of knowing the area better than his adversaries.

Two backlit silhouettes appeared—Yosh and Mr. Zanz. Linus stepped back warily, trying to figure out whether Yosh was being coerced by Mr. Zanz or whether he was coming of his own free will.

"Don't worry, Linus!" Yosh called out as he approached. "We're alone! Mr. Zanz has things to tell you."

Linus glanced at his watch again. Everything seemed to be under control. He relaxed slightly as Mr. Zanz and Yosh came closer.

"Good evening, Linus." Mr. Zanz looked tense. "I'm terribly sorry for everything that's happening. I owe you an explanation. Are Chem and Mieg with you?"

Linus shrugged and dodged the question. "Why are we meeting here?" he asked.

"It's a location you're completely familiar with, plus I thought it would be better to meet in the Protected Zone. It's more difficult for them to act here than in our area."

"Who do you mean by 'them'? Your friends the cops?" Linus muttered between clenched jaws.

"Wait!" Yosh broke in. "We were wrong. Mr. Zanz is just as trapped as we are. He's on our side."

Linus studied Yosh's face, not knowing whom to trust anymore.

"That's the truth," Mr. Zanz continued as he glanced around worriedly. "When you first hooked up to my network, everything was going well. We'd had a few close calls, as we always do when exam period approaches, but they weren't serious. We were in full command of the situation."

"What kind of close calls?" Linus asked.

"The electronic police," Mr. Zanz explained. "They have expert teams on the lookout for transfers between realms. Up to now they've never been able to corner us."

"And now?" Linus pressed him.

"Well, actually, it's much more alarming than I thought. The people who came to see me—the ones Yosh heard through the door—are threatening me. They've successfully infiltrated my organization by passing themselves off as renegades. They found out we were planning something. But I've managed to convince them I'd collaborate with them."

Mr. Zanz adjusted his eyeglasses. He was sweating so profusely they slid down his nose. Yosh took Linus by the arm.

"I believe him," he said. "You've got to as well."

Linus winced, undecided. "What makes you believe him?"

Yosh turned to Mr. Zanz, who nodded. Then, looking Linus straight in the eye, Yosh said, "Yesterday, Mr. Zanz came down to see me in a panic. He wanted to warn me that people were going to come by to question and arrest me. I didn't believe him at first. But I didn't want to take any risks. He convinced me to hide. We took cover behind the garbage cans. And that's when I understood. Two men came knocking at my door. When no one answered, they broke it down."

Yosh started trembling like a leaf.

Mr. Zanz continued for him. "They searched every

inch of the Bresco apartment. Then they went upstairs to my place and ransacked everything. Yosh and I have stayed away from the building since yesterday. We've moved in with a member of my network, someone I trust one hundred percent."

Linus was in shock. He didn't know what to say.

"I tried to buy time," Mr. Zanz explained. "The other night, when they saw you in the warehouse office, Linus, they wanted to arrest you. I convinced them to wait because there wasn't sufficient evidence. I had to play a double game, understand? But now I've exhausted their patience and have no more leverage. It's very important for you to know one thing: they can make arrests only prior to the exam. That's why they're in such a rush. If the two of you make it and get tested by the Great Processor, they can't challenge the result. You can imagine the outcry if people realized fraud was possible."

Yosh had pulled himself together now. "Where are Chem and your sister? We have to warn them."

Linus snapped out of his stupor. "They're not far. I . . ." He looked at his watch and cried out, "We've been discovered!"

WARNING was flashing in luminous letters on the tiny screen. Mr. Zanz turned pale. Just then, cries echoed in the adjacent street.

"Hurry!" Linus said. "Follow me!"

He raced to the school gate, followed by Mr. Zanz and Yosh. Mr. Zanz gave them a push to help them over, then jumped and swung himself up. He had just enough time to straddle the gate and jump down on the other side before three shadows charged down the blind alley. A man called out, "Stop! Zanz, we know you're there!"

Linus grabbed Yosh by the arm and they ran through the school courtyard. Mr. Zanz followed closely behind. Soon they were swallowed up by the nearly pitch-black darkness.

"This way!" Linus whispered.

The threesome turned into a covered playground, almost stumbled over a flower planter, bypassed a building, and tore down a stairway leading to the rear exit. They latched on to the gate leading to the concrete passageway. Their lungs on fire, they swung over it and ran down the passageway until they were out on the boulevard. There Chem and Mieg, both breathless and panic-stricken, were waiting for them under a glowing streetlamp.

"Mr. Zanz isn't a traitor!" Linus said, panting. "Hurry up! The others are right behind us!"

"We have no choice," Mr. Zanz said, pressing his ribs to relieve his pain from running. "You'll have to come hide with us at my friend's house."

Immediately all five started running together, zigzagging their way through the pedestrians on the boulevard, with Mr. Zanz in the lead.

"But how did they find us?" Chem asked as they ran. "How could they have known we would . . ."

Mr. Zanz stopped in his tracks. The others did too. "You think it's me?" he asked, looking straight at Chem. "You think I told them?"

Chem didn't reply. He eyed Mr. Zanz, who was shorter than he was, with scorn.

"Well, I didn't!" Mr. Zanz yelled in Chem's face. Then he turned to Mieg, apparently struck by something. "What did that woman say when she met you outside school?"

"Nothing. She gave me a swipe card," Mieg said.

"A swipe card! Where is it?"

"Here," Linus said, feeling his legs weakening. "In my pocket."

"Chuck it into the nearest trash can!" Mr. Zanz ordered. "That's how they've been tracking us."

"Of course, the card!" Chem said, angrily. "I should have detected it! What an amateur!"

"You couldn't have," Mr. Zanz said, comforting him. "Their nanochips are hermetic."

Linus pulled the card out of his wallet and was on the verge of throwing it into a trash can when he stopped in midair. "I have a better idea," he said. "Over there!"

Card in hand, he rushed to the tram station on the opposite side of the boulevard. For a moment he was hidden from view by a tram that had stopped to pick up passengers. When the tram started up again, Linus reappeared, standing on the sidewalk, a broad grin on his face. "Let's go," he said. "The card will travel instead of me. I stuck it in the frame of an advertising panel."

Mr. Zanz smiled. "A good way to lose them."

"And if they track us down again," Chem whispered to Linus, "we'll know for sure Mr. Zanz is taking us for a ride."

After running another hundred yards, they went into the station entrance and disappeared into the crowd and lights of the underground system.

• • •

Several hours later, hiding safely at the house of Mr. Zanz's absent friend, they took stock of the situation. Things certainly looked gloomy.

"You can't hole up here for eleven days until the exam," Mr. Zanz said. "Your parents will go to the police. And you can't possibly miss school."

"Then we might as well give up," Yosh said.

"Giving up isn't an option." Mr. Zanz removed his eyeglasses. "There's only one solution: every shred of evidence against you has to be destroyed and we have to behave as if none of it ever existed."

"What do you mean by 'none of it'?" Linus asked.

"My organization. I have to trash it, wipe it out, delete it. It's the only solution. Without evidence, the Internet security police can't make arrests. If we delete all the computer memory files, their assignment concerning us will be terminated. No one will have the right to spy on us anymore. That's the law, and for once, it's to our advantage. I'll contact the members of my network tonight and order them to erase everything."

The four young people were speechless. They were sitting around a big kitchen table. In front of them, a bowl of barely touched ravioli was getting cold. None of them had any appetite. Mieg couldn't seem to get warm, even huddled against Yosh, and he didn't dare move. Chem, his elbows on the table, shook his head, unwilling to accept defeat. "So all our efforts will have been for nothing?" he asked.

"We have to face the facts," Mr. Zanz replied. "My organization had already been infiltrated. It was doomed. What I want to avoid is you boys bearing the brunt of this. Let me repeat myself: without evidence, they can't arrest you. It will be as though we never existed."

Linus looked at Chem. "I'm sorry I dragged you into this," he muttered, sadly.

"It's destiny, Cookie," Chem said, smiling. "Just think, I almost succeeded!"

Mr. Zanz got up. He had a strange expression on his face. "Chem is truly a computer genius," he declared. "The truth is, you could have succeeded without my help. I shouldn't have offered the support of my network."

Mieg sat up. "Are you saying it's still possible?"

Mr. Zanz nodded. "Of course it's still possible. How do you think I did it twenty years ago? I was alone. I did it without anyone's help. I was just determined to choose for myself what I wanted to do with my life. I didn't care if I made a mistake; I was ready to suffer the consequences. I wanted to safeguard what I feel makes us human, thinking beings—the capacity to decide, choose, and act."

He walked across the kitchen. "I'm going to start the deletion process. We anticipated a special code for this, so it won't be that complicated. As a general rule, it's always easier to destroy than to create." Mr. Zanz went into the other room, leaving behind him a worried silence.

"What's on your mind, Linus?" Yosh asked.

"I'm thinking about my future," Linus answered without raising his eyes. "With everything that's happened recently, I almost forgot why I originally wanted to cheat on the exam."

Yosh nervously shifted his position on the bench. "I didn't," he said.

Linus sent him a distressed look. He was the only one who knew about Yosh's mysterious brother, the only one who understood Yosh's true motivations, not to mention his genuine suffering. Leaning against Yosh's shoulder, Mieg yawned, struggling to stay awake. "If everyone just behaved and stayed where the Great Processor assigned them, everything would be much simpler," she mumbled. "Though it's not completely fair."

"Mr. Zanz has failed in his attempt to improve things," Linus said in an unfaltering voice. "But he tried. And all may not be lost. Networks can be replaced, can't they?" He turned to Yosh. "Before meeting you and Mr. Zanz, I had no plan. But now I know what I want to do."

He sprang from the bench and started pacing around the kitchen, muttering to himself. Then he loudly and distinctly said, "Me in Realm Two, Yosh and Mieg in Realm One, Chem in Realm Three. If we found a way of staying in touch, we could create a clandestine super-network. See what I mean?" Linus stopped and leaned against the refrigerator door. He broke into an enigmatic smile and added, "Our time as little merry-go-round horses is over."

While the others stared at him wide-eyed, Linus envisioned his destiny. He was convinced that beyond the wall that had been blocking his path and causing him such anguish three months earlier loomed a large fallow area, a stretch of wasteland on which everything had yet to be built.

"If Chem is still willing," he said, "we'll take the exam our way!"

Chem smiled. "I have just enough time to mess with the Great Processor's internal clock mechanisms," he declared. "For the swap to work, the data has to be exchanged the very second it's being entered."

"And what if it doesn't work?" Yosh asked, anxiously.

"You just keep your respective scores."

"Is that all?"

"Yes. Well . . . they would certainly figure out someone had been trying to cheat. And they may even trace it back to me. But I don't care. I'm already excluded from their system no matter what."

Linus bit his lip. "Can't you program something for yourself?"

Chem brought his hand to his scarf and started laughing. "My place is in Realm Three, Cookie. I've told you that a thousand times. I'm known for my 'rebellious spirit.' It's in all my files. Even my parents are aware of it. They have no illusions. If I were to fall on a crackpot who wanted to exchange his score with mine, I'd refuse. I am fully prepared to pay the consequences for my acts. But that won't stop me from giving them a hard time."

"I wonder how I could ever have thought this was a fair system," Mieg said.

"It's because you didn't know anyone from the other realms," Yosh said, gently. "You probably thought we were all monsters."

Chem jumped onto the bench, startling Mieg. He began to growl like an animal and scratch his armpits.

"Woof! I'm the scary rebel from Realm Three!" he said. "A bloodthirsty, dangerous wild beast! Grrr! I'll eat you alive."

Then Linus started dancing around the table like a demented person. "I'm a native from Realm Two!"

"You're both stupid," Mieg said, blushing.

"You're right!" Yosh cried out. "As soon as I get to Realm One, I'll have all of these guys locked up."

Meanwhile, in the room next door, Mr. Zanz was e-mailing the coded message specially created for circumstances such as this one to all members of his organization. He was startled by the sudden peals of laughter coming from the kitchen. Then he smiled. In an hour or two, twenty years of work would go up in smoke. That was the magic of computers: everything could be erased.

As for the human beings involved, they would have to silence their memories, at least temporarily.

Mr. Zanz was convinced his sacrifice would not be in vain. Flowers could sometimes grow from a mound of ashes.

I'm sure these four kids are outstanding gardeners, he thought as he rubbed his eyes.

chapter 20

D-DAY MINUS 5

On a sunny Sunday afternoon in early spring, the Hoppes were entertaining friends in their garden. The Wolfs had come with their two children: Ewen, a seven-year-old boy, and Ismène, a girl who was the same age as Linus. Two other couples with no children had been invited as well. Mr. Hoppe wore a straw hat to protect his head through his thinning hair from the ultraviolet rays of the sun, and lay stretched out in a deck chair with his eyes half closed. The lunch had been abundant and delicious, washed down with wine labeled *traditional* for the adults, and now Mr. Hoppe was under the spell of a pleasant lethargy.

Mrs. Hoppe cheerfully confided to her friend Frida Wolf that her husband had never been much of a drinker. "When we were younger," she said, "regulations still allowed a high alcohol content in beverages. So in those days, it was routine that he'd fall asleep after just one glass."

Little Ewen had settled in the living room with his 3-D game console. Linus paced around the terrace, agitated and at loose ends, like a lion in a cage.

"How about lending Ismène a bike?" Mrs. Hoppe suggested. "You and Mieg could go down to the pond with her and show her around."

Linus shrugged. "I don't feel like it."

"Well then, I don't know . . . why don't you play cards?" Mr. Hoppe suggested from under his hat.

"Cards?" Linus winced. "What a drag!"

The adults around the table started laughing. In her corner, Ismène was sucking on a lock of her hair.

"Or how about helping Mieg fix dessert?" Mrs. Hoppe said. "I'm sure she could use a bit of help."

"Fine with me," Ismène said, timidly.

"Linus will go with you," Mrs. Hoppe added, encouragingly. And as Linus dragged his feet, leading Ismène to the kitchen, Mrs. Hoppe whispered in Frida's ear, "I can't wait for the exam to be over so that I can see Linus smile again. I don't know about Ismène, but Linus has been in a bad mood for months."

"Well, don't expect my mood to get better!" Linus grumbled under his breath as he overheard his mother's comment.

"What did you say?" Ismène asked, following right behind him.

"Nothing."

In the kitchen, they found Mieg in a panicked state. She was tearing at her hair and peering into a recipe book. The table looked like a battlefield, with eggshells and candied fruits strewn about like decimated armies.

"Oh, no! Oh, no!" Mieg was ranting. "I mixed in the butter much too soon! It's not going to come out right!"

"Can we help you?" Ismène asked.

"Certainly not!"

Mieg bumped into Linus as she got near the stove, almost burning herself with the cake pan.

"Why did I ever choose this stupid recipe?" she moaned in despair when she saw the cake. "This cookbook is lame."

"It's Grandma's recipe book," Linus pointed out. "You shouldn't criticize it."

Just then, the giant computer screen in the living room lit up and beeped to signal that someone wanted to get in touch. Linus poked his head through the doorway and used the remote control to accept the connection. Grandma's jovial, round, suntanned face appeared on the plasma screen.

"Mieg, you're in luck; it's Grandma. You'll be able to tell her what a high opinion you have of her book," Linus said, laughing.

"She's come onscreen to check on me," Mieg said, wiping her hands on a dish towel. "I told her I would try to bake her cake."

Linus, Mieg, and Ismène left the kitchen and stood in front of the monitor.

"Hello, Grandma!" Linus and Mieg said.

"Hi, kids!" Grandma greeted them playfully. "How is your day going?"

"Badly!" Mieg barked back.

"Is it because of my cake?"

"Yes!"

"Maybe I can help with a long-distance salvage operation?" Grandma offered. "Tell me what's wrong."

"It's no use. It's too late."

Grandma sighed and wrinkled her nose. "What's the weather like over there?" she asked.

"It's sunny here, Mrs. Hoppe," Ismène said, butting into the conversation even though it was none of her business.

"Sunny . . . hmmm . . . But it probably rained last night."

"Yes, Grandma, it did," Mieg confirmed, curious about what her grandmother was driving at.

"Well, that explains it all, darling!" Grandma said. "This cake can't take humidity. It isn't your fault. Does the dough feel viscous?"

"Yes," Mieg said.

"And, tell me, was the flour slightly coagulated?"

"Yes!"

"Then it's what I thought," Grandma said, making her diagnosis in a solemn voice. "I see only one solution: leave the dough in the oven for fifteen minutes at a very low temperature. Careful, though. It must not bake! Then take it out, knead it again, and bake it until it's done."

Mieg's face brightened. "Thank you, Grandma. You're great! I'm going straight back to the kitchen."

"Can I help?" Ismène asked again.

"Sure. You'll be my assistant."

The two girls headed out of the living room, leaving Linus in front of the screen. Ewen was playing with his console in the background, oblivious to the rest of the world.

"Well, Linus dear," Grandma said. "You're the one I wanted to talk to. How are you?"

"I'm okay," Linus lied.

"I hope your parents aren't driving you too crazy with your exam."

Linus shrugged. "They're convinced I'll do well."

"And what do you think?"

"I have no idea."

Grandma rubbed her cheek. "I think you're admirable," she said. "So much pressure on a person your age. It's no good. But I see you're facing up to it."

Feeling more confident, Linus asked, "How was it, before? When you were my age?"

"This may not be the best time to tell you about it," Grandma said, smiling. "Things were completely different."

"I'd like to know."

"I wasn't tested by the Great Processor, since it didn't exist at the time," Grandma said. "But though I feel this system is worse than the former one, things were by no means ideal then. Children were given the same schooling up to the age of fourteen or sixteen. After that, those who didn't get good grades were assigned to specialized training programs. The others went to high school and took final exams. These exams were corrected by teachers, which I guess wasn't considered very objective. That's why it was decided to replace the teachers with the omnipotent processor. The essential thing, for you, is to know what you want."

Linus agreed, but kept his lips sealed.

"Do you know what you want?" Grandma asked.

"Yes, I do," Linus admitted. He was tempted to tell her everything. The words were on the tip of his tongue. It would be such a relief to confide in his grandmother and get her support. "I want . . . ," he started. "I want what's best for me, and . . ."

Grandma raised an index finger to her lips. "Shhh! Don't tell me! I know you're clever enough to get what you want, and I have confidence in you. We shouldn't talk too much over the Internet. When it's all over, write to me by postal mail."

"In the old-fashioned way?"

"Yes, exactly." Grandma chuckled. "It's like Mieg's cake. Slow and costly, but all the more flavorful."

"Well, we'll report on the cake after we've eaten it," Linus said. Then he blew his grandmother a kiss and logged off. He returned to the kitchen, feeling more lighthearted. He could have sworn that his grandmother had guessed everything and approved of his decision.

• • •

"Here's the dessert!" Mieg announced, making her triumphant appearance on the terrace, followed by Ismène and Linus.

She was holding a platter with a splendid-looking cake, fresh from the oven.

"My mother's cake!" a jubilant Mr. Hoppe said with excitement. "It takes me back to my childhood."

A murmur of admiration rippled through the gathering of adults, all of whom were lounging on deck chairs. It was a marvelous day.

Mieg set her creation on the table. "Ismène and Linus were excellent assistants," she said. "I hope the end result will match our efforts."

"How prescient!" Ismène's father smiled. "Let's hope that the success of the cake foreshadows your two assistants' success on the exam five days from now."

"Hear! Hear! Let's drink to Ismène's and Linus's scores," Mr. Hoppe proposed, pushing his hat back, like a cowboy in an old-fashioned Western.

"Good idea!" Mrs. Hoppe exclaimed.

Mieg glanced at her brother, somewhat embarrassed. But Linus was smiling, looking serene and proud in front of the cake, a glass of mango juice in his hand.

Ismène followed his example and lifted her glass. Then she announced, "If Linus and I are both admitted into Realm One, maybe we'll eventually get married."

A peal of laughter ran through the gathering, and Linus blushed deeply. Mieg was giggling uncontrollably. While everyone clinked glasses, Linus mentally heaved a giant sigh of relief. Ismène's silly comment had just provided him with an added reason for flunking and getting assigned to Realm Two.

• • •

That night, after the guests had left, Linus received Chem's message, followed by Yosh's. They were brief and innocuous-looking and appeared on Linus's screen at around nine o'clock. Their content wasn't important, but each was a sign that everything was moving ahead as planned. Chem was a few days behind schedule, but not disastrously so. The main thing left to do was fine-tune his program for exchanging data in real time. According to the messages, neither Yosh nor Chem believed they had been watched since the night Mr. Zanz had dissolved his organization. And none of them had been in touch with Mr. Zanz.

Linus often thought back to his last conversation with Mr. Zanz, when all of them had taken refuge in the apartment of a renegade. While the others had slept, Linus had gotten out of bed. He'd found Mr. Zanz sitting on the bench at the kitchen table. Together they had finished the dish of ravioli in silence. Then Linus had told him about his decision. Mr. Zanz had listened, looking at Linus attentively with his green eyes.

"I wish I still had your enthusiasm." He'd sighed. "Though, if you want, I'll help you. Who knows? We may yet accomplish great things together."

Linus had nodded eagerly. He couldn't possibly imagine then what his life would be like after the exam, but the knowledge that he could count on a friendly presence in Realm Two gave him courage. He and Mr. Zanz had stayed in the kitchen together until daybreak.

• • •

From the drawer of his desk, Linus took out the album in which he had filed away all the documents—photos, e-mails, and drawings—Yosh had sent him during their weeks online. He left his room and knocked on Mieg's door. She was busy working. Architectural blueprints were spread out on her drawing board. Linus knew that even though his sister found manual work without computer assistance a real chore, she somehow always met her professors' expectations.

"Sorry for disturbing you," Linus said.

"Come in."

"I got confirmation from Chem and Yosh," he announced, sinking down on Mieg's bed with the album.

Mieg looked up and listened, her pencil suspended in midair above the sheet of paper.

"Good," she said. Then, without another word, she finished tracing a line with her ruler.

Linus was baffled. "Is that all you have to say?"

"What more is there to say? That's it. It's over. We'll just have to wait for the fateful moment."

Linus leaned back with his hands behind his neck. "One thing is sure. I won't ever get to marry Ismène Wolf. And that's no great loss."

Mieg laughed. "True, but you may never get to meet a lot of the awesome girls who'll be admitted into Realm One," she pointed out.

"Girls like you?"

"Obviously I didn't mean me."

"I know. It was my way of telling you I think you're pretty awesome," Linus said, softly. "I'm really sorry for thinking I couldn't trust you." He handed Mieg the album. "I'd like you to keep this for me. You can read it or not read it; I don't care. But I'd like you to hide it for a time."

Mieg took the album and, without opening it, got up and stashed it inside her closet, under a pile of notebooks. "We'll hardly get to see each other," she said with a lump in her throat. "I'd be lying if I said this made me happy."

"I try not to think about that too much," Linus said.

"Today was our last Sunday with Mom and Dad."

"Probably."

Linus turned toward the wall. "At least you can go on seeing Yosh. I'm glad the two of you get along."

Mieg nodded, tears rolling down her cheeks. "I like him a lot," she said. "But then I think about Mom and Dad. It'll be dreadful for them when you're gone. They aren't at all prepared for you to leave and—"

"Stop!" Linus pleaded. "The three of you have the required accreditation, so you'll be able to come see me—that is, if Mom and Dad aren't too disgusted at having a son in Realm Two. It's Chem I'm worried about. In Realm Three . . ." He gestured, chasing away his dark thoughts. Then he added, "We'll see. If anyone can find a way out, it's Chem."

Linus got up and gave Mieg a kiss on the cheek. "I

made a decision," he declared in a strong, determined voice. "I understand I have to do something with my life. There's nothing sad about this. The worst thing that could happen now is for Chem's program to fail. After everything we've done, if I end up in Realm One, it'll be a major setback."

By the time he left Mieg's room, Linus felt very much like a parachutist about to make his first jump—both terrified and exhilarated.

D DAY

"Phew!" Mr. Hoppe said, coming into the kitchen. "What a horrible night!"

He sat down next to Linus, who was paralyzed with apprehension and staring at the full glass in front of him. When he put a hand on Linus's shoulder, Linus jolted as if he'd been given an electric shock.

"Careful! Calm down, Linus. You almost spilled the shake," Mr. Hoppe said, easily measuring his son's anxiety at ten on a Richter scale of fear.

Linus had dark circles under his eyes and an ashen complexion. It was only six in the morning, but the whole household was up and bustling.

"I slept very badly," Mr. Hoppe said. "Your mother, on the other hand, never even went to bed, as far as I know."

"No comment," Mrs. Hoppe grumbled. She was kneeling on the floor, her head inside the oven.

"Could you please tell me what you're doing?" her husband asked.

"As you can see, I'm cleaning the oven."

"At six in the morning?"

"Yes, at six in the morning. Is there a law against that?" Mrs. Hoppe popped her head out of the oven and straightened. She was holding a sponge, her features were drawn, and she too had rings under her eyes.

"I guess there aren't any bylaws for this kind of behavior," Mr. Hoppe chattered, seemingly afflicted with nervous talkativeness. "In fact, who would ever think of addressing manual cleaning, when your oven is programmed to clean itself?"

Mrs. Hoppe looked at her sponge absentmindedly. Then she glanced at Linus and plunged her head back into the oven. It seemed that the mere sight of her son gave her an overwhelming desire to scrub.

Mr. Hoppe cleared his throat and fiddled with his bowl, moving it to the left and then away from the edge. He thumped his fingers on the table. "Where's Mieg?" he asked.

"In the bathroom," Mrs. Hoppe answered, her voice echoing in the oven cavity. "She's been there at least an hour."

"Fine, fine . . . ," Mr. Hoppe remarked. "And how are you, Linus? Feeling all right?"

"Please keep your voice down," Linus said, softly. "I have a headache."

"You can't!" Mr. Hoppe cried. "You can't have a headache today, of all days. Please drink your shake. And stick an aspirin patch on. Two, if need be!"

Linus picked up his glass with a shaking hand and moistened his lips. "I can't," he said.

"Come on, Linus. You need some nutrition. You can't take the exam on an empty stomach. That's the last thing anyone would recommend."

"Why?"

"Well, because . . ."

"Because what?"

"I can't tell you; you know that. The examinees aren't supposed to know anything about the exam conditions. It's an important part of the evaluation. But you should eat something."

Mrs. Hoppe extricated herself from the oven. "I couldn't swallow a thing on the day of the exam," she said. "I was like you, Linus. All tensed up. The mere smell of food turned my stomach. But that didn't prevent me from being admitted into Realm One—and quite easily, actually."

"Don't encourage him!" Mr. Hoppe said, his temper flaring. "Eating would keep him busy and take his mind off things. But do what you want, Linus. I, for one, am going to make myself a gigantic breakfast."

"Good! That way you'll talk less and it'll be a relief for us all!" Mrs. Hoppe snapped back as she threw her sponge into the trash can. "Now I think I'll clean the windowpanes."

• • •

At eight-thirty, the Hoppes climbed out of their car. Exam day was one of the rare occasions when Paris was clogged with traffic jams, because the exam center was located in the eastern Open Zone, which meant that all the examinees had to be escorted by family members, regardless of their driving clearances.

"What a madhouse!" Mr. Hoppe complained. "Look at this mess!"

The spacious esplanade surrounding the exam building was overrun by the crowd. Cars were parked chaotically, and people swarmed like flies in front of the center's heavy, majestic door. The examinees were engulfed by a teeming mass of parents, uncles, grandparents, brothers, sisters, all in various states of stress. The youngest members of the families dodged around the legs of their elders, at the risk of getting lost in the crowd.

Linus was astounded by the sight. He'd never imagined such a crowd. His hope of finding Chem and Yosh before the exam was completely unrealistic. It would be impossible.

"Let's get closer," Mrs. Hoppe suggested.

They started pushing their way through the crowd single file. "Pardon me, excuse me, sorry if I stepped on your toes." Mieg, looking pale as death, walked just behind Linus. Since coming out of the bathroom, her face puffy and her eyes red, she had not said one word. Linus didn't resent her for it. He sensed that mental telepathy was allowing them to communicate with each other, and that the things they were saying transcended what could be expressed with words.

Mr. and Mrs. Hoppe stopped just as they reached the stairs to the center. Mrs. Hoppe hugged Linus tightly.

"They'll be opening the door very soon. Will you be all right?"

Linus looked at her, overcome with emotion.

"I understand," she said. "But you'll see, a few hours from now, it will all just be a vague memory."

"You won't even remember why you were so anxious," his father added, to reassure him.

A sudden commotion rippled through the crowd. Standing on tiptoe, Mr. Hoppe announced, "I guess it's time! They're opening the door!"

He clasped Linus in his arms so tightly he almost smothered him. "Whatever happens," he mumbled into Linus's ear, "I'll always be proud of you!"

Linus felt his heart melting. His father had tears in his eyes. Linus had never seen him so upset before. Unable to say a word, he hugged his mother and kissed Mieg. Then he joined the flow of examinees heading for the entrance. He turned to wave to his parents and sister and called out, "I love you!" Swallowing hard, he forced himself to add, "See you later!" Then he climbed the stairs in a daze.

Just before plunging into the building, Linus looked at the sky. It was pale, whitish blue, still slightly hazy from the morning humidity. The black façade of the center seemed to rise several miles above Linus, like an arrow planted in a blue expanse.

• • •

Inside the monumental, marble-lined lobby, it was surprisingly silent. Hundreds of teenagers Linus's age were huddled against each other like terrified animals. Linus looked around, hoping to catch sight of Chem and Yosh, but it was a waste of time.

The silence was disrupted by a strident whistle and the sound of a throat being cleared near a mike. Everyone looked up at the balcony jutting over the lobby. A man in a suit, flanked by a dozen attentive men and women, looked at the crowd of examinees. Linus felt a stab in his heart when he recognized the young, short-haired woman from the night of the demonstration. Quickly he lowered his head to avoid being noticed by her.

The man at the mike began to speak. "Welcome, everyone, to the examination center. We all know how important this day is in determining your future. As of today, the die will be cast: you will be leaving the world of childhood and becoming full-fledged citizens. In the future, one of you may even have my job! Others among you will have to go live far away from your families and build something new. Lastly, some of you—and I sincerely hope this won't happen to too many—will have to be excluded from society because you will be judged incapable of being integrated into it. Whatever the outcome, you will have to assume it is for your own good, the good of your families, and the good of society as a whole. We appeal to you: please be scrupulous in obeying the rules so that the exam can take place under the best possible conditions."

Linus looked at the balcony and saw the speaker surrender the mike to a younger man who was holding a sheet of paper in his hand.

"The children whose last names begin with the letters *A, B, C, D* are to go to the far end of the lobby and take the stairway to the floor below," the man said. "Those whose names start with *E, F, G, H* are to take the stairway on the right to the second floor."

Instructions were still being given, but the crowd in the lobby was growing restless. Linus worked his way to the right-hand staircase and went up to the second floor with his peers. His mind was a blank as he followed along mechanically. The E, F, G, H group reached a long corridor where rows of leather padded doors seemed to extend around the building. Perplexed, the group came to a halt in front of the first door. There was a name posted on it: Ebhert, Octavio.

"Is that someone in our group?" a short girl asked, scowling.

"Yes, it's me," a skinny boy said. "My name is Octavio Ebhert."

One by one the names posted on the doors were read out loud, and little by little the group dispersed as each person found his or her door. Linus was among the last to make his way down the impressively long, serpentine corridor. At last he stopped in front of his name and turned the doorknob.

"It's locked," said a girl in orange overalls who was waiting outside the door nearest his. "I wish it would never open. I have an urgent need to pee. It's awful. Don't you?"

"No," Linus mumbled.

He was glad to hear a voice come over the loudspeaker. "The second-floor examinees are in position. Permission is granted to open the doors. Please go in and shut the door behind you. The exam cannot begin until all the cubicles are securely closed."

Instantaneously all the doors unlocked with a click. Linus turned toward the girl in the overalls. "Good luck!" he said.

She shrugged. "Luck is useless. There's no way of cheating with the Great Processor."

"You're right," Linus said, hastily. "I was thinking of your need to pee."

He opened his door and shut it behind him.

The cubicle was dark and very narrow. In the middle he saw a seat, or rather a kind of capsule, mounted on pneumatic jacks anchored to the floor.

"Sit down!" an electronic female voice commanded.

Linus hesitated momentarily. He checked the sides of the capsule. They seemed smooth.

"Sit down right there!" the voice commanded more firmly. A beam of light shone down on the capsule from the ceiling.

Linus settled into the capsule. At least it was comfortable.

"Welcome to the exam," said the voice, now in a syrupy tone. "There is nothing for you to do or say. Our method of evaluation is completely painless."

All of a sudden Linus felt a helmet descend over his head and adjust to fit his scalp. Steel handcuffs popped out from each side of the capsule and clamped down on his wrists so that he could no longer move them.

"Relax," said the voice. "The helmet is equipped with electrodes to analyze your reactions. Electrodes will be applied to your torso as well."

A second later, a metal plate, fastened to an arm with moving joints, placed itself on Linus's chest. In spite of himself, Linus felt his breathing become more rapid.

"Open your mouth," commanded the disembodied voice. "We are going to place two nanosensors on the insides of your cheeks. It is completely safe and painless."

Linus grunted from the sensation of having two robotized tweezers enter his mouth. As soon as the sensors were in place, the tweezers withdrew. Completely unable to move, Linus began to sweat. He was on the verge of panic and had no time to analyze the situation. The light beam switched off, plunging the cubicle into total darkness.

Linus's heart now pounded uncontrollably. This wasn't anything like what he had expected. Whenever he'd thought of the exam, he'd pictured himself in a lecture hall, facing an army of teachers and having to answer questions on a screen with an optical pen. The reality didn't come close. Never had he imagined such isolation or darkness.

"The exam may begin," said the female voice.

The wall in front of Linus retracted with a swish and was replaced by a brightly lit screen. Linus squinted at it, but no clear image appeared. He was then blinded by a series of light flashes. Imprisoned by the helmet, he couldn't look away from the screen. Linus gasped. An image appeared—of himself! The photo dated from his second birthday. He was seated in front of a cake, blowing out candles. The photo that followed had been taken by his father, during a vacation at the seashore. Linus saw himself paddling in the waves and smiling. He had a keen recollection of the cool waves foaming around his legs. The memory took him so far back, he started feeling disoriented. More photos flashed by in rapid succession. They showed Linus at important stages of childhood: sitting on a swing, behind the handlebars of his first bicycle, proudly brandishing his first lost tooth . . .

Linus was torn between laughter and tears, but had no time to give in to any emotion. He felt fragile and vulnerable. His personal life was on exhibit before him and nothing seemed to belong to him anymore.

Now new types of images were interspersed with the family photos. They flashed onscreen for only a hundredth of a second, but long enough for Linus to glimpse a landscape with ruins, a cathedral, a bouquet of flowers, an airplane, a crowd in a sports arena, a storm, broken glass, and a man with a wrinkled face lying on a hospital bed. Every once in a while, in the midst of this chaos, Linus recognized himself, forever smiling, ever older, and frozen in a kind of artificial, remote happiness.

From inside the cubicle walls, sounds Linus couldn't hear very distinctly—breathing, voices, explosions, notes played on a violin, the roar of a train, the cries of a child, the meowing of a cat, the banging of a door—emanated. They blended into one another, amplified and grating, while the images onscreen flashed by more and more quickly. Then a strong smell of gunpowder filled the cubicle. It was unbearable. Linus was overcome by a wave of nausea. He wanted to scream, but lacked the strength; he was assaulted by ever more violent sensations. A metallic taste made him grimace; a shriek pierced his eardrums; a red image startled him. Suddenly he felt wet. Panicked, he wondered if he had urinated on himself, and started to writhe in his seat. But the sensation was cut short, replaced by strong heat, as though he were sitting on a scorching radiator. On the screen he saw a line of women cradling babies in their arms, race cars from the previous century, a rocket at liftoff, a garden in winter, an orchestra, a girl on crutches, a dark painting, and stars. A sugary taste now spread through his mouth, provoking a brief smile. Then, at the very same moment, he felt excruciating stomach pains, and a voice (was it his father's?) yelled into his ear, "You ate too many candies!"

Dazed by the pain, Linus began to groan. He was no longer in control of his mind, body, or emotions. He felt assailed by the screen, submerged in a relentless onslaught of noises, suffocated by the smell of dust and stagnant water, paralyzed by the brutal succession of hot and cold on his skin, and tormented with fear. His vision blurred with tears, but he lacked the willpower to shut his eyes and bring it all to a stop. Just as he sensed he might go mad, the screen went blank and the noises were silenced. All sensation drained out of him so completely that he felt emptied of his own substance.

"What is your name?" the synthetic voice asked.

Linus shuddered. He couldn't grasp the question. His brain had turned hard and inert, like a stone.

"What is your name?" the voice repeated.

To Linus, the words were shrouded in fog, and his thoughts were reduced to mush. "I . . . don't . . . understand . . . ," he uttered with difficulty.

"State your name!"

"Who . . . are . . . you?"

"Your name!"

Concentrating intensely, Linus managed to summon his recollections. He remembered now. He was at the examination center.

"Are you . . . the Great Processor?" he asked.

"Your answer!" yelled the voice.

The whirlwind in Linus's head dispersed, leaving a drafty emptiness. He was jolted by an electric charge running down his spine. He thought of Yosh. He wanted to yell, "I am Yosh Bresco!" but he remembered that they were not meant to exchange identities. If Chem's program worked, only his and Yosh's scores would be switched. Then, suddenly, like a drowning body resurfacing for air, Linus howled, "I am Linus Hoppe!"

An explosion went off in the cubicle, followed by a shock wave that rocked his seat. Afterward, Linus heard a commotion of voices, laughter, and whistling in his ears. He felt as if his seat were speeding recklessly forward. Then a wall loomed in front of him, a wall so tall he couldn't see where it ended. The seat was heading straight for it, like a car being crash-tested. Linus shrieked with terror. At the moment of impact, he lost consciousness.

• • •

When he opened his eyes, Linus was no longer in the cubicle, and the helmet and electrodes had been removed. He was lying on a mattress on the ground, in a big hall. In spite of the darkness, he saw other examinees around him regaining consciousness.

Linus sat up and leaned on his elbows.

"The examinees in recovery zone number five are in the awakening phase," announced a man's voice over the loudspeaker.

Immediately a door opened at the far end of the hall and two people, a man and a woman, entered. They started walking among the students stretched out on the floor. The woman addressed them. "The exam is over for all of you here," she said. "You will soon be given the results. But first, there is one final formality."

She nodded toward the man, who walked over to the nearest mattress.

"We request that you take the tablet that is being handed out," continued the woman. "You have nothing to fear; it's not dangerous. Just a light energy booster."

The man stooped down near the student closest to him, then went on to the next, and so on, until he reached Linus. Linus took the tablet but let it rest in his palm. He hesitated. Then he slowly brought it up to his mouth. A dreadful odor made him grimace. It turned his stomach, and a burning sensation rose up in his throat. The tablet smelled of vanilla! It was as if he'd stepped into a cold shower: he woke up completely. The terrifying sensations of the exam flooded his mind in vivid detail. As the examinees around him all swallowed their vanilla pills without the slightest disgust, Linus peered into his hand. He couldn't bring himself to swallow the tablet. He decided to wait it out, even if it meant feeling sick a bit longer. And since no one was paying attention to him, Linus slipped the tablet into his pants pocket.

"Good." The woman spoke again, after all the examinees had been attended to. "The Great Processor has gone over the data. I now have the honor of handing you your envelopes."

She looked down at the list of E, F, G, H examinees and called out the names one by one. Octavio Ebhert, first on the list, rose from his mattress with difficulty. He was unsteady on his legs and took a few cautious steps toward the woman. She handed him an envelope without comment and without betraying the slightest emotion on her face. Octavio, pitifully skinny and pale, seized his envelope and staggered back to his mattress.

Linus watched the procession of examinees retrieve the envelopes that would determine their destinies. None of the envelopes were opened. The examinees' recent ordeal was such that they no longer had the curiosity to find out the results. They were visibly resigned to going wherever they were told to, relieved the exam was over. The girl in the orange overalls, the one who had had an urgent need to use the restroom, heard her name called out—Himbert, Adélie. She got up. Linus knew he was next. As he followed Adélie with his eyes, he noticed a big dark stain on the backside of her overalls. She didn't seem aware of it and walked shamelessly and limply toward the hand holding out her future. Linus controlled his burning indignation. How dare they make students degrade themselves this way? How dare they use fear to decide which students would make good citizens?

"Hoppe, Linus!" the woman called out.

Linus got to his feet. He felt worn out, not so much from fatigue as from outrage. His thoughts rushed to Chem and Yosh, and even Ismène, and he wondered how they were faring at that very moment. As he walked between the mattresses, he surveyed his classmates compassionately. Their prone bodies reminded him of defeated soldiers who had been struck down by an unknown enemy and were prepared to do anything as long as their lives were spared. When he reached the woman holding out his envelope, he checked his anger, lowered his eyes, and responded with a painfully extracted "Thank you."

He held the envelope between his fingers. He decided to behave like the others, so as not to arouse suspicion. Since he hadn't taken the tablet, he knew he needed to be especially careful. He returned to his mattress and sat down, making every effort to look as haggard as his companions.

The woman and man glanced around at the group. Seemingly satisfied, they announced that they were leaving and walked out. A strange silence reigned over the room. Some of the examinees had stretched out and shut their eyes again, balancing the envelopes on their stomachs. Others were sitting, arms akimbo, looking down at the envelopes indifferently.

Linus crawled over to Adélie Himbert. She was sitting on her mattress, staring into space. "Hey!" Linus mumbled. "Are you all right?"

The girl turned to him with a dull look.

"You had an accident," Linus told her. "You should ask for permission to change your clothes."

Adélie clearly didn't comprehend what Linus had said. So he changed the subject. "Are your parents waiting for you outside?" he asked.

The word *parents* seemed to resonate in Adélie's mind. She opened her mouth. "My parents . . . ," she said, echoing him.

"I'm sure mine are very worried," Linus said, to keep her attention. "They must be impatient to find out my score."

"My score . . . ," the girl repeated.

Linus frowned. Somehow Adélie had been struck nearly dumb.

Linus heard paper being ripped behind him and

someone saying, "One hundred sixty-five." He turned toward the voice. It belonged to the short, scowling girl who had earlier led the group through the corridor. She seemed to be in full possession of her faculties again.

"One hundred sixty-five?" Linus said. "You've been accepted into Realm One. Congratulations!"

The girl stared at him, baffled. "Into Realm One . . . ," she muttered.

A murmur ran through the group as everyone finally regained their senses.

"So?" Linus said, encouragingly. "You must be happy."

A wan smile crossed the girl's face. "I don't know," she said. "I thought . . . well, I didn't expect . . ."

Other envelopes were being unsealed in every corner of the room, and each time, the brief sound of ripped paper was followed by a number being called out.

"One hundred twenty!" someone said, sobbing.

"One hundred fifty-five!" another said, jubilantly.

"One hundred forty!"

"One hundred eighty!"

There was a feverish agitation among the examinees. Amid the jubilant cries and sobs, Linus stared at his own envelope. The short, scowling girl tugged at his sleeve and pointed at Adélie, who was taking the sheet out of her envelope with a trembling hand.

"What's your score?" Linus asked, gently.

"There isn't one," Adélie replied.

Linus leaned over her shoulder.

"It must be a mistake!" Adélie cried out.

Linus was dismayed to read *Admitted into Realm Three* and, in very small print, *160, subject to reeducation.*

"I don't want to go!" Adélie sobbed.

Everyone stared at her. A boy with a smug expression on his face rattled off the rules like an official. "You have to accept your score. It's for your own good, the good of your family, and the good of society as a whole."

"But why?" Adélie moaned. She had fallen back on her mattress in despair.

"The fact that you ask that question proves you have to be reeducated in Realm Three!" shouted the same boy.

By now, almost all the examinees in group E, F, G, H had opened their envelopes. The only exception was Linus, who still wavered. *I too am a rebel,* he thought. *The Great Processor has surely detected it, and I'll be sent to Realm Three, with Chem. Possibly even with Yosh. In that case we're completely done for. There'll be no possibility of changing this disastrous outcome.*

The scowling girl looked at him persistently. "Well, are you going to open it?" she said, impatiently. "Or are you afraid of telling us where you're being sent?"

The others sniggered.

"Maybe he's been assigned to Realm Four!" someone said, giggling. "With the mentally sick. Look at him! He looks weird!"

Linus lowered his eyes. *Let's get it over with,* he thought. And holding his breath, he ripped open the envelope quickly.

"One hundred forty."

The three numbers danced before his eyes. "One hundred forty," he said again. "Admitted into Realm Two."

chapter 22

When group E, F, G, H came out of the big hall, Linus trailed at the end of the stream of examinees. He had an arm around Adélie Himbert's shoulder. She was crying inconsolably. The others, whether proud or humiliated, relieved or terrified at the thought of having to leave home, had accepted their scores and were walking alone.

Arrows pointed to the exit. The group treaded noiselessly through a series of corridors with closed doors. Linus shuddered at the mere sight of them, knowing what he and the others had all been through. He thought of the next year's examinees, whose turn would come to be brutally ranked by the Great Processor. He also thought back on all the years in school during which no one was ever told anything about the exam. As his father had aptly stated, the surprise effect was part of the evaluation.

"The poor kids!" Linus said under his breath. "They don't know."

Octavio Ebhert, who had been admitted into Realm One and was walking ahead of him, turned around. "What are you mumbling about?"

"I'm thinking about the kids who'll be put through this next year. I feel sorry for them."

Octavio shrugged. "It's really not that bad."

"I doubt you would have said that when you first came out," Linus shot back, surprised.

"I felt perfectly fine," Octavio said.

Linus frowned and fell silent. Octavio didn't appear to be bragging. He seemed sincere. Could it be that he had already forgotten the pain, the fear, the exhaustion, not to mention the feeling of having been stripped naked by a heartless machine and reduced to putty like a blubbering fool? Linus fondled the vanilla tablet in his pocket. A dreadful suspicion came over him. What if the tablet wasn't just an energy booster?

After passing the last arrow, the group flowed into a big lecture hall where other examinees were gathered. They were sorted at the entrance.

"Admissions to Realm One on the left!" announced a fat man with a mustache. "Realm Two on the right. Realms Three and Four, do not enter!" He directed operations with his fat arms, pushing back and separating the new arrivals.

Adélie clung to Linus. "Don't leave me!" she begged. "I'm frightened!"

Linus didn't have the chance to console her. The guy with the mustache was in front of him. "Your score!" he barked.

Linus handed him the sheet, and the man sent him to

the right, pulling him away from Adélie. She cried out in despair.

"Good luck!" Linus shouted. "If you meet a boy by the name of Chem Nogoro, tell him you saw me!"

Adélie disappeared, having been pushed back outside the lecture hall. Inside, Realms One and Two stood opposite each other, staring at each other like strange beasts. Surrounded by the Realm Two crowd, Linus got up on tiptoe, trying to find Yosh on the other side.

Suddenly he spotted a familiar face in front of him. It was Ismène! She was among the students admitted into Realm One. Linus waved his arm to attract her attention. Ismène smiled at him spontaneously and waved her hand to greet him. Then her expression darkened. A deep incomprehension was written on her face. Linus, on the other hand, continued to smile. He simulated applause to congratulate her on her score. Ismène blushed and turned away. She edged toward the back rows, where she promptly vanished from Linus's line of vision.

He sighed. *What a stupid girl!* he thought, feeling slightly hurt even so. *Just five days ago she wanted to marry me!*

He shrugged off his humiliation and looked for Yosh again. His attention was drawn by shouts at the entrance door, where the mustached guard was still sorting out the examinees.

"Linus! Linus!" someone shouted.

Linus felt his heart stop. It was Chem.

"Over here!" Chem yelled, jumping up and down.

Linus pushed his way through the crowd. "Chem! Here I am!" he shouted back. But by the time Linus reached the door, Chem had disappeared. Linus grabbed the guard by his jacket. "Where did the boy who was calling my name go?"

"You mean the boy who was yelling? I threw him out. Come on now! Move on!"

"But why?" Linus asked boldly.

"Realm Three pests are not allowed here!" the guy grumbled. "Move on, I said!"

Linus stared at the door, incredulous. Up to the end, he had hoped Chem would avoid Realm Three. With tears in his eyes, he went back to his section of the lecture hall. And what if everything had failed? What if his score and Yosh's had not been switched? What if 140 was his own score and not Yosh's? *After all, it's possible,* he thought, *that I'm not that exceptional. Just average . . . Because I was living in Realm One, I assumed I was on the same level as the rest of my family. It was an illusion. My parents must have brought me up thinking I was better than I am because they couldn't contemplate anything else.*

Now Linus didn't even dare look for Yosh. He hid within his section, indifferent to everything and deeply melancholic. Next to him, however, two girls were poking each other with their elbows and giggling as they appraised those who had been admitted into Realm One.

"Look at that one," one girl said. "He's cute! What a shame for us."

"And that girl!" her friend said. "She looks like a Christmas gift, with those ribbons in her hair!"

Linus wanted to put his hands over his ears so he could block out the two busybodies.

"Look! Up there, on the right! An extraterrestrial!"

"Where?"

"Over there! The guy with the moon face and spiky hair."

"Yes!" said the other one, jumping up and down. "I see him! You're right, that's some hairstyle!"

Linus looked up. "Where?" he shouted to the girl. "Where's the moon face and spiky hairstyle?"

The girl pointed, and Linus spotted Yosh. Sure enough, there he was, his strange looks already out of place. Jubilant, Linus gesticulated to attract his friend's attention and called out, "Yosh! Yosh!"

Yosh saw him, and his face lit up with a smile.

"He's not that ugly when he smiles," conceded one of the two giggly girls.

Linus squeezed his way to the edge of his section to talk to Yosh. Though separated by several yards, they faced each other, beaming.

"Bravo!" Linus shouted above the din.

"Thank you!" Yosh shouted back. Then, wrinkling his nose, he asked, "How much?"

Linus used his fingers to indicate the three numbers.

Yosh's eyes widened. He apparently hadn't expected such a good score. Meanwhile, Linus waited to see *his* result, and when Yosh indicated 1-8-0 with his fingers, Linus instantly felt relieved.

Just then, a strident whistle sounded and the lecture hall fell silent. A door opened at the far end of the Realm One side.

"Those admitted into Realm One are requested to leave the hall," said a voice over the loudspeaker. "You will be given new ID cards."

Yosh didn't move. He was pale and looked into Linus's eyes. Then he was swept along by the flow of the crowd.

"Send my love to Mr. Zanz!" he called out to Linus. "I hope we'll see each other again!"

Linus lunged forward with his whole body. "Send my love to Mieg!" he shouted in reply. "We *will* see each other again!"

He watched as Yosh disappeared behind the heavy door sealing off Realm One. All alone, Linus stood in a daze, realizing with terror that they might not meet again for months, years, or even . . . ever. What was in store for him now? What was the procedure for the newly admitted? Where would he be spending the night? Where would he be living and with whom? Linus had no idea what to expect. From now on, it wasn't just his future that was hazy; it was the present too. He surveyed the empty section opposite. Had he made the right decision?

A door opened on the Realm Two side of the room, and the voice on the loudspeaker gave out new instructions.

"Those admitted into Realm Two are requested to leave the hall. You will be given new ID cards."

Now Linus Hoppe was swallowed up by the crowd. He disappeared behind a door, into the great unknown of his new life.

Linus Hoppe is now living in Realm Two—and it's not at all what he thought it would be. If he wants to see his family and friends, he's got to regain hope and the will to fight for his freedom.

Anne-Laure Bondoux's companion book,
The Second Life of Linus Hoppe,
will be available in October 2005.
Here's a preview. . . .

The ambulance wove through deserted streets and boulevards. The streetlights filed by the windows. Linus looked at them pensively: if he succeeded in escaping the director's surveillance and becoming free again, he promised himself that he would do everything he could to save Chem.

Suddenly Toscane chuckled with satisfaction. "In four days my father will finally understand I'm not the person he thinks I am," she said. "I'm not like him. I'll never be like him!"

She locked her hands together, extended her arms forward, stretched like a cat, and cracked her knuckles. It was silent once again inside the vehicle, except for the glass flasks clinking in their boxes. Leaning his forehead against the windowpane, Linus tried to sort out the questions swirling in his head. So many things had yet to be explained. Suddenly his heart started to race. He had just realized something. "If I don't go back to the home," he said, "I'll be considered a deserter."

Toscane nodded, slightly embarrassed.

"I don't understand," Linus said. "I'll be wanted, put on file, and actively pursued by the police?"

Toscane nodded again. Anguished, Linus addressed Dr. Ambrose. "But then I'll spend my life in hiding, won't I? That's not what I had in mind! Not at all! I—I just wanted to live in Realm Two. I . . ." He broke off and bit his lip. He felt like a trapped rat. Everything had happened so fast he'd had no time to think about the consequences of an escape. In fact, he hadn't even been given a choice.

"You didn't warn me!" he wailed. "You said I was free, but that's not true. It's a lie! Even without the tracking bracelet, I . . ." He coughed, holding his throat with both hands.

Toscane shrank in her seat. Dr. Ambrose put a hand on Linus's back. "Nothing went as planned," she said gently. "We told you, the Internet police arrested members of the old organization. That was on the day of the exam. Since then, surveillance has intensified on every level. We think the police are investigating downgraded students. That would explain the extended period of time in transit homes. If you had stayed in the home, the police would no doubt have come to question you, and we had no way of protecting you there."

Linus felt completely crushed. Dr. Ambrose looked at him, commiserating. "Some people may have talked before they were killed," she went on. "Mr. Zanz was afraid the authorities might work their way back to you."

"Trust us," Toscane pleaded. "This escape was the only solution for you—and for all of us."

The ambulance slowed and drove alongside a building complex. Dr. Ambrose looked out the window. "We've arrived," she announced.

Linus sat up, deeply anguished. If he stepped out of the ambulance, he would automatically become a deserter, and his entire future would be jeopardized. He still had one alternative: he could ask to return to the home and wait to be assigned to a foster family. But how long would that take? And what if Toscane was right? What if the police could prove he had cheated on the exam? And what if they realized Yosh didn't belong in Realm One? And what if they discovered Chem was the mastermind behind the exchange? Linus suddenly felt the crushing weight of responsibility. One false step and he put the lives of his friends in jeopardy.

ABOUT THE AUTHOR

Anne-Laure Bondoux was born near Paris in 1971. She has written several novels for young people in varied genres and has received numerous literary prizes in her native France.